Other books by James Riordan

The Young Oxford Book of Football Stories
The Young Oxford Book of War Stories

Korean Folk-tales
Pinocchio
Gulliver's Travels
King Arthur
Sweet Clarinet
The Prisoner
When the Guns Fall Silent
Russian Folk-tales

The Young Oxford Book of Sports Stories

The Young Oxford Book of

Sports Stories

James Riordan

OXFORD
UNIVERSITY PRESS

For my sporting American cousins
FX, June, and Ann

OXFORD
UNIVERSITY PRESS

Great Clarendon Street, Oxford OX2 6DP

Oxford University Press is a department of the University of Oxford.
It furthers the University's objective of excellence in research, scholarship,
and education by publishing worldwide in

Oxford New York

Athens Auckland Bangkok Bogotá Buenos Aires Calcutta
Cape Town Chennai Dar es Salaam Delhi Florence Hong Kong Istanbul
Karachi Kuala Lumpur Madrid Melbourne Mexico City Mumbai
Nairobi Paris São Paulo Shanghai Singapore Taipei Tokyo Toronto Warsaw

and associated companies in Berlin Ibadan

Oxford is a registered trade mark of Oxford University Press
in the UK and in certain other countries

This selection and arrangement copyright © James Riordan 2001

The moral rights of the author have been asserted

First published 2001

British Library Cataloguing in Publication Data available

ISBN 0 19 278172 3 (hardback)
ISBN 0 19 278173 1 (paperback)

1 3 5 7 9 10 8 6 4 2

Typeset by AFS Image Setters Ltd, Glasgow

Printed in Great Britain
by Biddles Ltd, Guildford and King's Lynn

Contents

Introduction

Our aim in choosing the stories and poems for this book is, quite simply, to provide young people with a good read. Yet it isn't *that* simple. Sport is for girls as well as boys. As Oscar Wilde once reminded us about football, tongue in cheek:

> 'Football is all very well as a game for rough girls, but it is hardly suitable for delicate boys.'

We therefore need women as well as men authors, women's as well as men's sports. All the verses and three of the stories in this book are by women. Some pit women against men, in swimming and pool; some pose problems that women face in playing the game according to rules written by men; some suggest power and solidarity that sport can give women.

Like nothing else, sport today is international. So our book covers a wide range of games played in all English-speaking countries: ice hockey as well as swimming, basketball as well as soccer, cricket as well as fishing, pool as well as running, body building as well as horse riding and gymnastics. The contributions come from Britain and Canada, the USA and the West Indies. Some authors are little known, some are world famous, like Ernest Hemingway, Margaret Atwood, and Alan Sillitoe.

Like sport itself, not all our stories feature winners. We can't *all* win. Some just do the best they can. Some, however, *must* win for a higher cause—like James Riordan's footballers (based on a true event). Some could win, but don't bother, like Alan Sillitoe's long-distance runner. Some do sport for the challenge—against nature or themselves—caving, body building, deep-sea fishing.

Sport is not always what it seems.

We have selected our stories and verses to entertain. More than that. They are meant to inspire you to play, to dream, to create yourself.

James Riordan

Women Who Run

yes, they do run.
traces of early morning sweat
trickle down slick backs,
heels tense, ready to let feet fly.

the mountains, mauve and unmoving
poke up in the distance,
rub their shoulders,
brace their stubbly chins against a matt sky;
women run
in the shadows of these mountains.

summer licks their toes
and drapes itself over tanned arms,
as women who run heave breaths
in accord with the banners of triumph.
from many cultures, race, and tongues
these free spirits
have found a common foothold
in womankind

because they run;
yes they do, they run.

freely and forever.

Laurel Starkey

The Lone Runner

ALAN SILLITOE

The pop-eyed potbellied governor said to a pop-eyed potbellied Member of Parliament that I was his only hope for getting the Borstal Blue Ribbon Prize Cup For Long Distance Cross Country Running (All England), which I was, and it set me laughing to myself inside, and I didn't say a word that might give them real hope, though I knew the governor anyway took my quietness to mean he'd got that cup already stuck on the bookshelf in his office among the few other mildewed trophies.

'He might take up running in a sort of professional way when he gets out,' and it wasn't until he'd said this and I'd heard it with my own flap-tabs that I realized it might be possible to do such a thing, run for money, trot for wages on piece work at a bob a puff rising bit by bit to a guinea a gasp and retiring through old age at thirty-two because of lace-curtain lungs, a football heart, and legs like varicose beanstalks. But I'd have a wife and car and get my grinning long-distance clock in the papers and have a smashing secretary to answer piles of letters

sent by girls who'd mob me when they saw who I was as I pushed my way into Woolworth's for a packet of razor blades and a cup of tea. It was something to think about all right, and sure enough the governor knew he'd got me when he said, turning to me as if I would at any rate have to be consulted about it all: 'How does this matter strike you, then, Smith, my lad?'

A line of potbellied pop-eyes gleamed at me and a row of goldfish mouths opened and wiggled gold teeth at me, so I gave them the answer they wanted because I'd hold my trump card until later. 'It'd suit me fine, sir,' I said.

'Good lad. Good show. Right spirit. Splendid.'

'Well,' the governor said, 'get that cup for us today and I'll do all I can for you. I'll get you trained so that you whack every man in the Free World.' And I had a picture in my brain of me running and beating everybody in the world, leaving them all behind until only I was trot-trotting across a big wide moor alone, doing a marvellous speed as I ripped between boulders and reed-clumps, when suddenly: CRACK! CRACK!—bullets that can go faster than any man running, coming from a copper's rifle planted in a tree, winged me and split my gizzard in spite of my perfect running, and down I fell.

The potbellies expected me to say something else. 'Thank you, sir,' I said.

Told to go, I trotted down the pavilion steps, out on to the field because the big cross-country was about to begin and the two entries from Gunthorpe had fixed themselves early at the starting line and were ready to move off like white kangaroos. The sports ground looked a treat: with big tea-tents all round and flags flying and seats for families—empty because no mam or dad had known what opening day meant—and boys

still running heats for the hundred yards, and lords and
ladies walking from stall to stall, and the Borstal Boys
Brass Band in blue uniforms; and up on the stands the
brown jackets of Hucknall as well as our own grey
blazers, and then the Gunthorpe lot with shirt sleeves
rolled. The blue sky was full of sunshine and it
couldn't have been a better day, and all of the big show
was like something out of *Ivanhoe* that we'd seen on the
pictures a few days before.

'Come on, Smith,' Roach the sports master called to
me, 'we don't want you to be late for the big race, eh?
Although I dare say you'd catch them up if you were.'
The others cat-called and grunted at this, but I took no
notice and placed myself between Gunthorpe and one
of the Aylesham trusties, dropped on my knees and
plucked a few grass blades to suck on the way round.
So the big race it was, for them, watching from the
grandstand under a fluttering Union Jack, a race for the
governor, that he had been waiting for, and I hoped he
and all the rest of his pop-eyed gang were busy placing
big bets on me, hundred to one to win, all the money
they had in their pockets, all the wages they were going
to get for the next five years, and the more they placed
the happier I'd be. Because here was a dead cert going
to die on the big name they'd built for him, going to go
down dying with laughter whether it choked him or
not. My knees felt the cool soil pressing into them, and
out of my eye's corner I saw Roach lift his hand. The
Gunthorpe boy twitched before the signal was given;
somebody cheered too soon; Medway bent forward;
then the gun went, and I was away.

We went once around the field and then along a
half-mile drive of elms, being cheered all the way, and
I seemed to feel I was in the lead as we went out by
the gate and into the lane, though I wasn't interested

enough to find out. The five-mile course was marked
by splashes of whitewash gleaming on gateposts and
trunks and stiles and stones, and a boy with a
waterbottle and bandage-box stood every half-mile
waiting for those that dropped out or fainted. Over the
first stile, without trying, I was still nearly in the lead
but one; and if any of you want tips about running,
never be in a hurry, and never let any of the other
runners know you are in a hurry even if you are. You
can always overtake on long-distance running without
letting the others smell the hurry in you; and when
you've used your craft like this to reach the two or
three up front then you can do a big dash later that
puts everybody else's hurry in the shade because you've
not had to make haste up till then.

I ran to a steady jog-trot rhythm, and soon it was so
smooth that I forgot I was running, and I was hardly
able to know that my legs were lifting and falling and
my arms going in and out, and my lungs didn't seem to
be working at all, and my heart stopped that wicked
thumping I always get at the beginning of a run.
Because you see I never race at all; I just run, and
somehow I know that if I forget I'm racing and only
jog-trot along until I don't know I'm running I always
win the race. For when my eyes recognize that I'm
getting near the end of the course—by seeing a stile or
cottage corner—I put on a spurt, and such a fast big
spurt it is because I feel that up till then I haven't been
running and that I've used up no energy at all. And
I've been able to do this because I've been thinking;
and I wonder if I'm the only one in the running
business with this system of forgetting that I'm running
because I'm too busy thinking; and I wonder if any of
the other lads are on to the same lark, though I know
for a fact that they aren't.

Off like the wind along the cobbled footpath and rutted lane, smoother than the flat grass track on the field and better for thinking because it's not too smooth, and I was in my element that afternoon knowing that nobody could beat me at running but intending to beat myself before the day was over. For when the governor talked to me of being honest when I first came in he didn't know what the word meant or he wouldn't have had me here in this race, trotting along in shimmy and shorts and sunshine. He'd have had me where I'd have had him if I'd been in his place: in a quarry breaking rocks until he broke his back. At least old Hitler-face the plain-clothes dick was honester than the governor, because he at any rate had had it in for me and I for him, and when my case was coming up in court a copper knocked at our front door at four o'clock in the morning and got my mother out of bed when she was paralytic tired, reminding her she had to be in court at dead on half past nine. It was the finest bit of spite I've ever heard of, but I would call it honest, the same as my mam's words were honest when she really told that copper what she thought of him and called him all the dirty names she'd ever heard of, which took her half an hour and woke the terrace up.

I trotted on along the edge of a field bordered by the sunken lane, smelling green grass and honeysuckle, and I felt as though I came from a long line of whippets trained to run on two legs, only I couldn't see a toy rabbit in front and there wasn't a collier's cosh behind to make me keep up the pace. I passed the Gunthorpe runner whose shimmy was already black with sweat and I could just see the corner of the fenced-up copse in front where the only man I had to pass to win the race was going all out to gain the half-way mark. Then he turned into a tongue of trees and

bushes where I couldn't see him any more, and I couldn't see anybody, and I knew what the loneliness of the long-distance runner running across country felt like, realizing that as far as I was concerned this feeling was the only honesty and realness there was in the world and I knowing it would be no different ever, no matter what I felt at odd times, and no matter what anybody else tried to tell me.

The runner behind me must have been a long way off because it was so quiet, and there was even less noise and movement than there had been at five o'clock of a frosty winter morning. It was hard to understand, and all I knew was that you had to run, run, run, without knowing why you were running, but on you went through fields you didn't understand and into woods that made you afraid, over hills without knowing you'd been up and down, and shooting across streams that would have cut the heart out of you had you fallen into them. And the winning post was no end to it, even though crowds might be cheering you in, because on you had to go before you got your breath back, and the only time you stopped really was when you tripped over a tree trunk and broke your neck or fell into a disused well and stayed dead in the darkness forever. So I thought: they aren't going to get me on this racing lark, this running and trying to win, this jog-trotting for a bit of blue ribbon, because it's not the way to go on at all, though they swear blind that it is. You should think about nobody and go your own way, not on a course marked out for you by people holding mugs of water and bottles of iodine in case you fall and cut yourself so that they can pick you up—even if you want to stay where you are—and get you moving again.

On I went, out of the wood, passing the man leading without knowing I was going to do so. Flip-flap, flip-

flap, jog-trot, jog-trot, crunchslap-crunchslap, across the middle of a broad field again, rhythmically running in my greyhound effortless fashion, knowing I had won the race though it wasn't half over, won it if I wanted it, could go on for ten or fifteen or twenty miles if I had to and drop dead at the finish of it, which would be the same, in the end, as living an honest life like the governor wanted me to. It amounted to: win the race and be honest, and on trot-trotting I went, having the time of my life, loving my progress because it did me good and set me thinking which by now I liked to do, but not caring at all when I remembered that I had to win this race as well as run it. One of the two, I had to win the race or run it, and I knew I could do both because my legs had carried me well in front—now coming to the short cut down the bramble bank and over the sunken road—and would carry me further because they seemed made of electric cable and easily alive to keep on slapping at those ruts and roots, but I'm not going to win because the only way I'd see I came in first would be if winning meant that I was going to escape the coppers after doing the biggest bank job of my life, but winning means the exact opposite, no matter how they try to kill or kid me, means running right into their white-gloved wall-barred hands and grinning mugs and staying there for the rest of my natural long life of stone-breaking anyway, but stone-breaking in the way I want to do it and not in the way they tell me.

Another honest thought that comes is that I could swing left at the next hedge of the field, and under its cover beat my slow retreat away from the sports ground winning post. I could do three or six or a dozen miles across the turf like this and cut a few main roads behind me so's they'd never know which one I'd taken;

and maybe on the last one when it got dark I could thumb a lorry-lift and get a free ride north with somebody who might not give me away.

But no, I said I wasn't daft didn't I? I won't pull out with only six months left, and besides there's nothing I want to dodge and run away from; I only want a bit of my own back on the In-laws and Potbellies by letting them sit up there on their big posh seats and watch me lose this race, though as sure as God made me I know that when I do lose I'll get the dirtiest crap and kitchen jobs in the months to go before my time is up. I won't be worth a threpp'ny-bit to anybody here, which will be all the thanks I get for being honest in the only way I know. For when the governor told me to be honest it was meant to be in his way not mine, and if I kept on being honest in the way he wanted and won my race for him he'd see I got the cushiest six months still left to run; but in my own way, well, it's not allowed, and if I find a way of doing it such as I've got now then I'll get what-for in every mean trick he can set his mind to. And if you look at it in my way, who can blame him? For this is war—and ain't I said so?—and when I hit him in the only place he knows he'll be sure to get his own back on me for not collaring that cup when his heart's been set for ages on seeing himself standing up at the end of the afternoon to clap me on the back as I take the cup from Lord Earwig or some such chinless wonder with a name like that. And so I'll hit him where it hurts a lot, and he'll do all he can to get his own back, tit for tat, though I'll enjoy it most because I'm hitting first, and because I planned it longer.

I don't know why I think these thoughts are better than any I've ever had, but I do, and I don't care why. I suppose it took me a long time to get going on all this

because I've had no time and peace in all my bandit
life, and now my thoughts are coming pat and the only
trouble is I often can't stop, even when my brain feels
as if it's got cramp, frostbite, and creeping paralysis all
rolled into one and I have to give it a rest by slap-
dashing down through the brambles of the sunken lane.
And all this is another uppercut I'm getting in first at
people like the governor, to show how—if I can—his
races are never won even though some bloke always
comes unknowingly in first, how in the end the
governor is going to be doomed while blokes like me
will take the pickings of his roasted bones and dance
like maniacs around his Borstal's ruins. And so this
story's like the race and once again I won't bring off a
winner to suit the governor; no, I'm being honest like
he told me to, without him knowing what he means,
though I don't suppose he'll ever come in with a story
of his own, even if he reads this one of mine and knows
who I'm talking about.

I've just come up out of the sunken lane, kneed and
elbowed, thumped and bramble-scratched, and the race
is two-thirds over, and a voice is going like a wireless
in my mind saying that when you've had enough of
feeling good like the first man on earth of a frosty
morning, and you've known how it is to be taken bad
like the last man on earth on a summer's afternoon,
then you get at last to being like the only man on earth
and don't give a bogger about either good or bad, but
just trot on with your slippers slapping the good dry
soil that at least would never do you a bad turn.

Now the words are like coming from a crystal-set
that's broken down, and something's happening inside
the shell-case of my guts that bothers me and I don't
know why or what to blame it on, a grinding near my
ticker as though a bag of rusty screws is loose inside

me and I shake them up every time I trot forward.
Now and again I break my rhythm to feel my left
shoulder blade by swinging a right hand across my
chest as if to rub the knife away that has somehow got
stuck there. But I know it's nothing to bother about,
that more likely it's caused by too much thinking that
now and again I take for worry. For sometimes I'm the
greatest worrier in the world I think (as you twigged
I'll bet from me having got this story out) which is
funny anyway because my mam don't know the
meaning of the word so I don't take after her; though
dad had a hard time of worry all his life up to when he
filled his bedroom with hot blood and kicked the bucket
that morning when nobody was in the house.

I'll never forget it, straight I won't, because I was
the one that found him and I often wished I hadn't.
Back from a session on the fruit-machines at the fish-
and-chip shop, jingling my three-lemon loot to a nail-
dead house, as soon as I got in I knew something was
wrong, stood leaning my head against the cold mirror
above the mantelpiece trying not to open my eyes and
see my stone-cold clock—because I knew I'd gone as
white as a piece of chalk since coming in as if I'd been
got at by a Dracula-vampire and even my penny-pocket
winnings kept quiet on purpose.

Gunthorpe nearly caught me up. Birds were singing
from the briar hedge, and a couple of thrushies flew
like lightning into some thorny bushes. Corn had grown
high in the next field and would be cut down soon with
scythes and mowers; but I never wanted to notice much
while running in case it put me off my stroke, so by the
haystack I decided to leave it all behind and put on
such a spurt, in spite of nails in my guts, that before
long I'd left both Gunthorpe and the birds a good way
off; I wasn't far now from going into that last mile and

a half like a knife through margarine, but the quietness I suddenly trotted into between two pickets was like opening my eyes underwater and looking at the pebbles on a stream bottom, reminding me again of going back that morning to the house in which my old man had croaked, which is funny because I hadn't thought about it at all since it happened and even then I didn't brood much on it. I wonder why? I suppose that since I started to think on these long-distance runs I'm liable to have anything crop up and pester at my tripes and innards, and now that I see my bloody dad behind each grass-blade in my barmy runner-brain I'm not so sure I like to think and that it's such a good thing after all.

I choke my phlegm and keep on running anyway and curse the Borstal-builders and their athletics—flappity-flap, slop-slop, crunchslap-crunch-slap-crunchslap—who've maybe got their own back on me from the bright beginning by sliding magic-lantern slides into my head that never stood a chance before. Only if I take whatever comes like this in my runner's stride can I keep on keeping on like my old self and beat them back; and now I've thought on this far I know I'll win, in the crunchslap end. So anyway after a bit I went upstairs one step at a time not thinking anything about how I should find dad and what I'd do when I did. But now I'm making up for it by going over the rotten life mam led him ever since I can remember, knocking-on with different men even when he was alive and fit and she not caring whether he knew it or not, and most of the time he wasn't so blind as she thought and cursed and roared and threatened to punch her tab, and I had to stand up to stop him even though I knew she deserved it. What a life for all of us. Well, I'm not grumbling, because if I did I might just as well win this bleeding race, which

I'm not going to do, though if I don't lose speed I'll win it before I know where I am, and then where would I be?

Now I can hear the sports ground noise and music as I head back for the flags and the lead-in drive, the fresh new feel of underfoot gravel going against the iron muscles of my legs. I'm nowhere near puffed despite that bag of nails that rattles as much as ever, and I can still give a big last leap like gale-force wind if I want to, but everything is under control and I know now that there ain't another long-distance cross-country running runner in England to touch my speed and style. Our doddering bastard of a governor, our half-dead gangrened gaffer is hollow like an empty petrol drum, and he wants me and my running life to give him glory, to put in him blood and throbbing veins he never had, wants his potbellied pals to be his witnesses as I gasp and stagger up to his winning post so's he can say: 'My Borstal gets that cup, you see. I win my bet, because it pays to be honest and try to gain the prizes I offer to my lads, and they know it, have known it all along. They'll always be honest now, because I made them so.' And his pals will think: 'He trains his lads to live right, after all; he deserves a medal but we'll get him made a Sir'—and at this very moment as the birds come back to whistling I can tell myself I'll never care a sod what any of the chinless spineless In-laws think or say. They've seen me and they're cheering now and loudspeakers set around the field like elephant's ears are spreading out the big news that I'm well in the lead, and can't do anything else but stay there.

But I'm still thinking of the Out-law death my dad died, telling the doctors to scat from the house when they wanted him to finish up in hospital (like a bleeding guinea-pig, he raved at them). He got up in bed to throw

them out and even followed them down the stairs in his
shirt though he was no more than skin and stick. They
tried to tell him he'd want some drugs but he didn't fall
for it, and only took the pain-killer that mam and I got
from a herb-seller in the next street. It's not till now
that I know what guts he had, and when I went into the
room that morning he was lying on his stomach with the
clothes thrown back, looking like a skinned rabbit, his
grey head resting just on the edge of the bed, and on the
floor must have been all the blood he'd had in his body,
right from his toe-nails up, for nearly all of the lino and
carpet was covered in it, thin and pink.

And down the drive I went, carrying a heart blocked
up like Boulder Dam across my arteries, the nail-bag
clamped down tighter and tighter as though in a
woodwork vice, yet with my feet like birdwings and
arms like talons ready to fly across the field except that
I didn't want to give anybody that much of a show, or
win the race by accident. I smell the hot dry day now
as I run towards the end, passing a mountain-heap of
grass emptied from cans hooked on to the fronts of
lawnmowers pushed by my pals; I rip a piece of tree-
bark with my fingers and stuff it in my mouth, chewing
wood and dust and maybe maggots as I run until I'm
nearly sick, yet swallowing what I can of it just the
same because a little birdie whistled to me that I've got
to go on living for at least a bloody sight longer yet but
that for six months I'm not going to smell that grass or
taste that dusty bark or trot this lovely path.

I hate to have to say this but something bloody-well
made me cry, and crying is a thing I haven't bloody-well
done since I was a kid of two or three. Because I'm
slowing down now for Gunthorpe to catch me up, and
I'm doing it in a place just where the drive turns in to
the sports field—where they can see what I'm doing,

especially the governor and his gang from the grandstand, and I'm going so slow I'm almost marking time. Those on the nearest seats haven't caught on yet to what's happening and are still cheering like mad ready for when I make that mark, and I keep on wondering when the bleeding hell Gunthorpe behind me is going to nip by on to the field because I can't hold this up all day, and I think Oh Christ it's just my rotten luck that Gunthorpe's dropped out and that I'll be here for half an hour before the next bloke comes up, but even so, I say, I won't budge, I won't go for that last hundred yards if I have to sit down cross-legged on the grass and have the governor and his chinless wonders pick me up and carry me there, which is against their rules so you can bet they'd never do it because they're not clever enough to break the rules—like I would be in their place—even though they are their own.

No, I'll show him what honesty means if it's the last thing I do, though I'm sure he'll never understand because if he and all them like him did it'd mean they'd be on my side which is impossible. By God I'll stick this out like my dad stuck out his pain and kicked them doctors down the stairs: if he had guts for that then I've got guts for this and here I stay waiting for Gunthorpe or Aylesham to bash that turf and go right slap-up against that bit of clothes-line stretched across the winning post. As for me, the only time I'll hit that clothes-line will be when I'm dead and a comfortable coffin's been got ready on the other side. Until then I'm a long-distance runner, crossing country all on my own no matter how bad it feels.

The Essex boys were shouting themselves blue in the face telling me to get a move on, waving their arms, standing up and making as if to run at that rope themselves because they were only a few yards to the

side of it. You cranky lot, I thought, stuck at that
winning post, and yet I knew they didn't mean what
they were shouting, were really on my side and always
would be, not able to keep their maulers to themselves,
in and out of cop-shops and clink. And there they were
now having the time of their lives letting themselves go
in cheering me which made the governor think they
were heart and soul on his side when he wouldn't have
thought any such thing if he'd had a grain of sense.
And I could hear the lords and ladies now from the
grandstand, and could see them standing up to wave
me in: 'Run!' they were shouting in their posh voices.
'Run!' But I was deaf, daft, and blind, and stood where
I was, still tasting the bark in my mouth and still
blubbing like a baby, blubbing now out of gladness that
I'd got them beat at last.

Because I heard a roar and saw the Gunthorpe gang
throwing their coats up in the air and I felt the pat-pat
of feet on the drive behind me getting closer and closer
and suddenly a smell of sweat and a pair of lungs on
their last gasp passed me by and went swinging on
towards that rope, all shagged out and rocking from
side to side, grunting like a Zulu that didn't know any
better, like the ghost of me at ninety when I'm heading
for that fat upholstered coffin. I could have cheered
him myself: 'Go on, go on, get cracking. Knot yourself
up on that piece of tape.' But he was already there, and
so I went on, trot-trotting after him until I got to the
rope, and collapsed, with a murderous sounding roar
going up through my ears while I was still on the
wrong side of it.

It's about time to stop; though don't think I'm not still
running, because I am, one way or another. The

governor at Borstal proved me right; he didn't respect
my honesty at all; not that I expected him to, or tried
to explain it to him, but if he's supposed to be educated
then he should have more or less twigged it. He got his
own back right enough, or thought he did, because he
had me carting dustbins about every morning from the
big full-working kitchen to the garden-bottoms where I
had to empty them; and in the afternoon I spread out
slops over spuds and carrots growing in the allotments.
In the evenings I scrubbed floors, miles and miles of
them. But it wasn't a bad life for six months, which
was another thing he could never understand and would
have made it grimmer if he could, and it was worth it
when I look back on it, considering all the thinking I
did, and the fact that the boys caught on to me losing
the race on purpose and never had enough good words
to say about me, or curses to throw out (to themselves)
at the governor.

Swimmers

We are sweatless
and weightless
purity personified
our rhythmic motion
comforting as we
unite with fluids
of our individual
and species birth.

Runners on roads
skiers on slopes
chasers of balls
we are grateful
you leave oceans
lakes and pools
for those knowing
how body merges
intimately with
perfect medium
so even those
unlucky or clumsy
everywhere else
glide and hide
gracefully into
crystal refuge

Ruth Harriet Jacobs

The Swimming Race

JENIFER LEVIN

'There you go, kid. Made of snow.'

Sarge stepped back to look at her. Grease moulded his hands into enormous white mittens and he shook some off, raised a shiny white index finger. Through her goggles she followed the deliberate line it drew in air until it pointed at the centre of his belly. He circled it, delineating that core area while he kept his eyes on her face—it was the only part of her left unoiled, so she appeared to be wearing mime make-up in reverse—and he could see by the blank look that she was concentrating. He raised his voice so she'd hear through the caps.

'Here's where it comes from, right? The oven here.'

She nodded carefully.

'Think solar plexus! Means sun network. Sun braids, twining out from the centre here, this little oven of yours, right?'

She nodded.

'I'm talking heat. *Heat.* Just zoom in on the sun right here and you're fine.' He could feel his heart pick

up pace a little. 'You've got it right here. All yours, understand, no one else's. Keep you good and warm in that water.'

Her mouth shut. He saw the oozy white line of her throat move as she swallowed. He hoped to hell she didn't throw up again, there wasn't a whole lot more of her breakfast left.

'Hey!' He jammed his finger straight up towards the sky and she snapped to attention. 'Get right into your pace. Stay there and keep it up no matter what and don't change a thing for anybody else, understand. Hit that pace and stay there.' He raised both fists over his shoulders. Grease spattered. 'Remember. Anyone tries to dunk you, kick their balls off. Knock their tits off. Whatever.' She grinned. So did he. 'Right!'

'OK, Sarge,' she said. 'I'm OK.'

Bodies specked the beach getting greased gold or white or black. Some of them just used Vaseline. Whatever gave you the mental boost—realistically speaking, it eventually washed off whatever it was, just a little sooner than the rest of you. Sarge watched her. Feet slightly apart, dripping into the ground. She swung her arms gently and lowered her head. Shut them out effectively, he knew.

Down towards the shoreline's centre Parisi gestured at his trainer. Above the tension, the bending and glinting grease of twenty-nine bodies shimmering against the backdrop of the bay that morning, his voice rose.

'About ready?' Tycho grabbed his shoulder.

He caught one last full look at her, head lowered, concentrating. 'What do her stars say today, Johnny?'

'It's a good time for short journeys.'

'You're kidding.'

'Nope. No such thing as kidding where the heavens

are concerned, you know that, maestro. She's fine.' He caught Sarge's expression for a disappearing second and saw the flash of vulnerability there, pressed his fingers deeper into Sarge's shoulder. 'She's been training with the best, I hear.'

'Right,' Sarge whispered.

Dorey looked slowly up at them. When she smiled it was slight, but calm. She raised a hand, fluttered it, then brought it to her forehead for a gentle salute.

Tycho gave her the thumbs-up sign. He winked, and again she smiled. She turned towards Sarge.

What filtered through the grease, caps, goggles, suits to her was that she'd become, for these minutes before starting, the core of his universe. He'd seen her go blank without knowing that what she was really doing was the thing she called house-cleaning. She'd taken a minute or so, swept the insides smooth as fresh-cut plywood. Now he was the one concentrating. He was concentrating on her. Dorey felt herself radiate. For Sarge, she gained stature, and while he watched felt the substance of her own power without having to dig deep for it. This quietly surging sense of strength gave two words to her: of course. *Of course* passed across the blank board in her head. She stood as tall as she was, and relaxed.

Both men pushed off in the escort boat. Its prow tilted further up while Tycho spun the motor to a low hum and took it out a fair distance, edged her slowly around in a half-circle so they had a full view. All twenty-nine were lining up on the embankment wall.

Sarge crouched in the dully rocking stern. He was all attention, gazing at the bodies lined there. They were still milling around a little, the count hadn't yet started. Towering above most of them was Parisi. His height and bulk made him swagger—Sarge had always

figured, though, that on a smaller man his movements
would have been tense, sudden. If he went out too fast
today he could be worn down around midway. If he
kept pace and used his brain then he'd pose a threat
later on. Sarge ticked them off one by one, went down
the line. Dorey was twelfth from the left. In the boat
Sarge half-stood and then he saluted, held the gesture
extravagantly in the air. If she couldn't see, no matter.
He'd done it mostly for himself anyway.

'She looks good!' He slapped knuckles against
Tycho's back, kept his eyes on shore. 'Looks good,
huh?'

Twelfth from the left, Dorey lowered her head
again, swung her arms back a little. Ready to fly.
She tensed, relaxed, then did something completely
different. She became a still, concentrated beam, a ray
of something, waiting to leap towards something else.
Air was the bridge spanning the distance between what
she'd become and what she'd leap into. Ten. Instantly
free of clutter, she was slate-blank, slippery snowlike
white on the outside, inside buzzing a consistent high-
pitched static. Nine. The body next to her crouched
low. She sensed rather than saw it, snapped invisible
blinders in place to either side. Seven. Six. Someone at
the line's other end had already jumped. Her guts
lurched and she froze into place, wait, wait, must wait,
be fair now, be fair. Four. Had she missed five. Three,
two.

She blasted with the gun, exploded into air and
arched swiftly down, smashed cleanly through water
surface with another explosion. This one she didn't
hear. She was inside it. She broke through, went down,
curved upwards spewing wild bubbles and that first
stroke wound up around and down into the water,
propelled her ahead and then another and another. The

water was clear, too cold to feel at first. You could only
gasp. She did. She yanked herself ahead furiously, kept
her arms on line with invisible pulleys that each hand
caressed in alternate rhythm. Dorey gasped to the side.
Stroked stroked stroked stroked stroked gasped to the
other side. Feet, arms, churned around her. She
sprinted for clear space.

'Right!' Sarge flung arms up, rocked the stern. He
choked with everything that swelled his insides out.
They were off, and with it he felt a gush of relief
before the immediate sharpening of tension.

Watching him, Tycho breathed again. 'Right,' he
said.

Dorey sprinted for open space because then she'd be
able to really swim. Needed room for that, lots of it. A
body edged up on her right and she pulled away,
imagined her arms like windmills alternately propelling.
She liked to imagine them making complete circles.
The water was cold and still and she was beginning to
feel it on her face, against her arms, so cold it seemed
to burn and the illusory tingling heat was invigorating.
Wake flutter-kicked ahead of her, to the side. Someone
rode her heels. She felt a stiff-fingered hand brush the
ankles, looking for a hold. Fingers tried to grip. Trying
to pull her under and bounce on ahead over her body.
She put her feet together. They blended in a tail so
they weren't feet any more but a melded lashing
organism at that opposite tip of her. She bent her knees
and the tail dipped, snapped up with her hips and
smashed into a face. No more grasping fingers.

She passed the body to her side. A woman. Time, she
told herself, time to settle down now. Forget the group
ahead. Around her near the surface the water was clear.
Look straight down and it was opaque, you couldn't see
the bottom but along it were mossy strings of colourless

plant reaching up, swaying with the dense current. Dorey slid through. Kept her arms like windmills spinning from the shoulder axis. She breathed steadily now with the roll of her body. The windmills weren't windmills but water mills. They pulled her along.

A B C D E she said, A B C D E. Ahead by several yards now several pairs of feet beat quickly just below the surface, six-beat, four-beat, gaining more distance on the rest. She settled for her pace right now. Figured the time she was making and figured she could pick up later when it got necessary. She ran through the alphabet again, got into numbers.

From the waiting boats, they'd looked like a flock of enormous birds taking off with a rush and flurry of wings, grease spewing the water in their wake like feathers left behind. Steadily, swiftly, the flock spread to something like hourglass shape—top-heavy and bottom-heavy. Then the top thinned and it was simply bottom-heavy. The pyramid pointed and at its point was Dorey, ahead of her a cluster who together made a big cherry on top of the cone spreading through water.

Dotting the bay to either side of them, escort boats hovered. One by one they shifted position, headed further out as the pack moved and spread. To Tycho they were mother birds clucking watchfully after their nestlings, each dip of an oar another chirp of anxiety. Each prow was a beak poking through glistening water, nosing among the passing capped heads to claim the one that belonged to it.

'Let's go.' Sarge stepped to the bow, balanced standing there. 'After her, that's my baby.'

The sun blazed a little higher. Eight o'clock. Sarge glanced back, then ahead, measuring. He'd be surprised

if this pattern held all the way through. The group ahead stuck like glue and pulled further away. Parisi, her main rival, wasn't one of them but that Australian woman whose name he kept forgetting was. He gave them another half hour at that pace, wondered when the few would start their kick away from the pack behind. That would be the first reckoning. They'd see then how well it worked, because his strategy with her had been simple. Let the ones in front erode themselves. Let the ones in back hold out and then put on sudden agonizing sprints. He'd thrown most of his eggs this time around into one basket: her pace. Except for that necessary scrambling sprint at the beginning, she'd just keep the same pace throughout. And if only she'd maintain this pace of hers, he knew she'd have some speed left at the end when things got rough.

The cluster of front-liners—Connery, Vanderhoff, Adams, MacIntyre, Beaujais, and Santosuelos—stayed there, the kickers he knew were in that crowd back there still hung back. Dorey'd hit her pace and, obediently, stringently, she was maintaining it. Occupied a unique place in the field. Grease was gliding from her arms, streaking the water white now with each stroke. Sarge counted. His pulse sped in sympathy. Sure looked good.

At eight thirty Connery and the Australian woman were battling it out with the others far ahead. Vanderhoff had fallen back and Dorey was gaining steadily on him. Another fifteen minutes and Sarge checked behind. Parisi'd started his breakaway. The format was changing, shifting back there. A thick-clustered wide sweep of bodies constituting the rear. A group of

several pulled away now, Parisi among them. Very slowly, they were gaining.

By nine she'd passed Vanderhoff. Sarge would have liked to stop her for a feeding but waited for a signal from her and there was none. He figured he'd have to trust her judgement this early on—she knew by how she felt now approximately what time it was. Lifting high, arching in that flamboyant, pointed spearing motion that pierced the water cleanly, her arms were bare of grease now and shimmered flesh-tone in the increasing expanse of sunlight. She kept it steady. Steady pace.

Quarter to ten and the water temperature dipped. At five to ten she stopped and tread. Tycho rowed them closer. 'Chocolate?' Sarge shouted.

'Uh-huh!' she was shouting too, louder than him. 'Hot!' Her hands shivered around the cup. She spilled it and the dark spread momentarily through that clear surface before vanishing. Her head was pounding in rhythm with the stroke she'd just halted, and she heard Sarge yell not to worry, more coming up.

Fog spread on the insides of her goggles. She dimly saw the stick coming towards her, an arrow blunted by the steaming cup which she grabbed with one hand while the other arm kept treading. Must modulate her grip now, tight enough to keep hold but loose enough so she didn't crush it. Mustn't drop it again, she told herself, this heat was important.

'Keep it up!' he leaned over port. 'You're damned good, lady.'

'What place?' she yelled.

Sarge lifted six fingers. He shouted out the number. Shouted not to worry, shouted keep it up, shouted listen for the whistle. Lips nipped the cup's rim and fluid curled into her mouth, sweet dark heat. She got it all down in two long gulps. Signalled towards the boat with a wave how good she felt, and Sarge gestured back, shouted something she couldn't quite make out except to know that it was encouragement. She continued. The water slapped cold around her and met with the fluid streaking an internal stream of warmth from her mouth to her stomach. With each stroke she got a little more lukewarm, then cooled with rapid certainty until everything was numb.

By ten thirty Parisi'd moved up to within a few hundred yards and was closing the gap slowly, slowly. At eleven Sarge saw him stop for a feeding and whistled her in, too. Bay's temperature had dropped again. The sun was riding high burning his shoulders and he shouted to her how did she feel.

'Huh?' she yelled back.

Just after eleven Connery was pulled from the water.

'How are we doing?' Tycho sounded cheerful. Sarge could almost hear him whistle as he rowed steadily, easily, working up a cool film of sweat in the afternoon heat. 'Captain?'

'Good. Watch for that Parisi though, I don't like it.'

Tycho leaned into it, leaned back with it. 'Mars is doing her a lot of favours right now, you know. And there's Venus sitting smack on top of her Moon. Everything's in working order.'

Someone else was being lifted from the water ahead. Sarge caught sight of a towel being wrapped, flashing

white in the sun like a truce flag. Another sorry flag
was unfolded, the body lifted again from the bottom of
the boat and cloaked. That Australian.

Sarge rummaged in the tarp for his slate. Checked
his pocket for chalk. 2 MILES, he scrawled. Whistled.
Whistled twice. Three four five times. Got to fifteen
before she stopped, shoulders and head bobbing out
uncertainly. Leaning over port so his entire naked torso
swung out, he held up the slate. Behind them Parisi'd
begun his sprint and was gaining rapidly.

'Now,' Sarge muttered, and Tycho held oars steady
in the water. 'Now the fun starts, right?'

How do you feel? he was yelling to her. She was
shaking her head, deaf. How do you feel? he shouted
until his voice went hoarse. Finally she pointed to her
head.

'Hurts,' she blurted.

On the stick he passed her some sustagen mixed
with aspirin. She got half of it down and Parisi swam
by them. 'Hold it,' Sarge hissed. Tycho listened. 'Hold
it, I know that swimmer, he won't keep it up.' Again
he held the board high. He shook another fist in the
air, and what spattered from his hands this time wasn't
grease but the bay's dampness and the dampness of his
own flesh.

'Go!' he howled. 'Go! Right!'

Dorey's head dipped, arms curved into action. The
oars did too.

A buoy marked the beginning of the last miles.
She'd picked up pace. So had the current. It warned of
a river mouth two miles away, riled the surface to small
waves, darkened the surface clarity to a texture that was
no longer crystalline. They'd been going for good time
all morning, gloriously undisturbed by the slightest
ruffle or rift. Except for the temperature, it might as

well be a pool. Now the water made them pay for that pleasure. As always. The group ahead had held a pace of two miles plus per hour. Currents built slowly against them from here on in. Towards the end they'd be slowed, and that water would be going against them at a rate equal to their best time. Pretty soon. Pretty soon now, Tycho would haul in the oars and cross them on the boat's floor like weary bed-mates. He'd hit the motor.

'Now,' Sarge counted her strokes. His own arms ached. 'Now, baby, now. For the good part.'

Eyes shooting from him to her to him again, Tycho grinned. He grinned at the unmistakable glee in the man's voice.

There was the voice that said if she did not get out now she would die. There was the voice that said if she gave up now she would die. Her strokes walked the tightrope between voices and, for lack of any other option, Dorey kept going.

Below the waist she was numb. Above the waist torn to shreds. Sun blasted the bay with the fresh light of Canadian spring. Later she'd see how it had burned her shoulders and back. Waves popped against her stomach, slapped back at her reaching hands.

There were two voices, two sections of her body. And she had two pairs of eyes. One was the set of goggles strapped securely around her head, the fogged pair that could no longer see much and no longer cared. The other was the set of eyes that left goggles behind, left the discomfort, this unfortunate circumstance in which her body found itself. These eyes focused in on the sun, gazed on flashing yellow light, blinked in the heat. Reaching. Saw silver twinkle from her fingertips

in the darkening rough pull of the water. Reaching. Closed and opened again and saw things ahead in the water that no goggles could have seen. Saw twirling blue and green and golden kaleidoscope segments glitter before them, went deeper into the puzzle of colours towards its centre, the core which at first was orange and then pink and then a blushing, shimmering scarlet before it became a black hole of nothing from which yellow burst like sunlight. Reaching. Again she blinked in the heat. Breathed and water came in. Breathed and this time air. P Q R S T. Nine thousand nine thousand one nine thousand two nine thousand three nine thousand four breath. Saw fish the colour of rainbows and thought that was pretty strange. Fish the colour of rainbows didn't breed in Quebec, did they? Uh-uh. She blinked and the heat gave shape to a human figure. It was Ilana. Ilana called her and she reached for the image. Then it changed to Sarge. I'm trying, she told him, I'm going as fast as I can.

'Hah!' Sarge howled glee. The water roughened. It slapped back at them and she kept going, groaned to the side with her body's roll and picked up pace even more. She was gaining on Parisi with the water swirling and breaking roughly now, smashing against them, and they were both gaining on the diminishing cluster of swimmers ahead. Second to last mile. The current made miniature foam-tipped pockets of whirlpool action all around. Tycho revved up the motor.

It was the beginning of the last mile, which was a mile upriver, against the currents. It was a twisting spider's web of water that tumbled rather than flowed.

Beaujais, local boy and the favourite, lunged. That was the only way to describe it—he lunged over some

vortex and broke ahead. MacIntyre went under, came up yards behind where he'd been.

Santosuelos's crew went in after him. Sarge watched towels wrapped again, swirling bright red and green in the afternoon sun, wrapped around and around, the boat's motor coughing with greater force as it headed for waiting ambulances on shore.

Ambulances waited among the crowd lining both banks. This last mile upriver was a real gut-buster. It made Sarge perspire and he felt himself swell near explosion with a massive diversity of prideful sensations and undefined desires. Made him want to try it again himself. His throat choked watching her take a swing at the current, boxing waves, slugging back at the battering ram of tide.

Beaujais had it. Just as he'd expected. Only for all his talk and all his image-boosting, Sarge had to admit that on a gut-level he'd never expected her to do so well. Looked like she'd place third now. He'd thought maybe sixth, seventh, eleventh, maybe first among the women if she were lucky, maybe second. He'd expected her to place and grab some of the money but not so near top prize. She'd surprised him too. And now that she'd surprised him the way she had, done so well up to this point, he wanted her to sprout water wings and soar past Parisi, show herself off to everyone there and teach them all a lesson in case they'd never learned it before. His breath flew away for a second. Like most new believers, he wanted the world to join him in this new-found revelatory ecstasy.

'Go!' he shouted at the top of both lungs. 'That's my baby! Now! Watch now, go for it, go for it, all right, Johnny. All right, Johnny, now for the real stuff, watch her now, watch and let's go for it. Hah! Go for it, lady!'

She made her plunge during a relative lull in the
flow. So did Parisi. Now he was putting on another
sprint and, leaning over the prow so spray soaked his
face, Sarge knew it was the last he'd be able to manage.
Thing was to match him now if she could. Match him
and keep him from struggling too far to a lead, that
way wear him down first.

It pounded against her. Crushing in, slamming
angrily, opposed to the rhythm of her heart. A long,
thick body sprinted now beside her. Dorey felt herself
flood with one final burst of hatred. Last sensation she
was capable of. Why, she sobbed, why. You bastard.
Some voice laid a bet that she'd never do it. The hell I
won't, she said. Because she had to, there wasn't any
choice, if there'd been one she'd have taken it. So she
threw in the extra that wasn't really there, poured
herself ahead by reaching. Nine thousand nine hundred
and ninety seven. X Y Z A B. Breath. She spit out
water and wanted to puke. She sobbed to the left. Five
strokes and again to the right. Kept it up, went numb
except for the infinite, increasingly loud boom-thump-
thump that began in her chest, rang in both ears,
pulsed along her neck and the feelingless subskin of
each wrist. Reaching. Ten thousand twenty-one. Threw
in the extra and felt herself go dry but held on to that
final deadly pace anyway, felt it dragging her forward
against the river's bloodstream, and in this way she
passed him.

Silver-grey sprayed in zigzag lines from her
fingertips, each hand a drill blasting through the barrier
of grey. Muted sparks flew back towards her face. It
was a tunnel now and she had no light or warmth.
Hard to move. Your arteries froze if it got cold enough.
Each hand a pointing, spearing icicle tip poking with
impossible slowness through the oncoming walls of

water. The tunnel filled in behind so there was no
going back. It closed in on each side, from the top,
from the even darker bottom. Sparks snapped at her
lips with each stroke. Ten thousand one hundred and
ninety-nine. B C D. Or was it R S T. Was it eleven
thousand now. Felt like night. It occurred to her then
that there was one way out of this mess and only one
way, and that was just to keep going. This barrier was
also a bridge. It was the only way. She took it. Set her
arms and hands to walking its planks.

The nasal, guttural murmurings and shouts of the
crowd lining both banks rose in volume. At the dock's
roped-in area Ilana, Dorey's best friend, and Tycho's
wife, waited, felt caught in a continually shifting
tornado of sound.

Ilana'd caught sight of Beaujais's face before the
ambulance doors swung shut. He was a fairly young
man, she knew, mid-thirties. What impressed her most
was the ageing effect of the swim—lines crawled across
his forehead, spread from eye corners across his cheeks
to connect with his mouth's shivering edges. The effect
was a greying one. She recognized it immediately,
telltale tint and markings of someone who had lasted
through something. She sat on the stack of blankets,
the stack of towels, crossed her legs, tapped her fingers
to some nebulous tune she was remembering. Ilana
wondered how long it would be now. She waited for
Tom MacIntyre, waited for Parisi.

She almost daydreamed. When she heard the
guttural humming roar pitch higher than before, bodies
twist and spring with tension around her, she caught
their rhythm in spite of herself and stood too, began to
move forward along the dock as if sleepwalking and her

cool fluidity increased in speed as she understood what
was happening. It was like that still, unbreathing
timeless space before springing from a cliff, that
moment when she began to see.

Thick-fingered, burly hands latched firmly around her
upper arms. Dorey couldn't feel them but knew she
was being lifted. Up. Out. Hands slid struggling for a
grip. Careful to swing her clear of the dock's edge.
She'd thought of something just then, something
important and she wanted to tell Ilana. Quick or she'd
forget it. When her goggles came off the sun made her
wince. Felt like she was lying there flat on her back on
the light-sprayed, heat-soaked wood of the dock, but
she knew she was still standing. How could that be.
Where was Ilana? Hurry or she'd forget. The thing
she'd thought of just now with the last fly of sparks
from that drill her left hand made. Cap came off. One
cap two cap three cap four. Inside a laugh started.
What was her time? Where was Ilana, now, now, quick
where was she. No good. Now she'd forgotten. Dorey
was on her back and she wanted to cry.

Did it, she said. Beat them all! Then she felt that
glow.

The stretcher's sides curved around her. Fog over
both eyes. Looking down, Ilana noticed that beneath
each eye was a pale half-circle of swelling and beneath
each swollen mound a deep red indented curve, like a
gash. The sun blinded. Dorey shut her eyes, opened her
mouth making sounds Ilana couldn't understand. On the
street of some city, Chicago maybe, Ilana'd seen a mother
shopping with her deaf son one afternoon. They'd been
speaking in signs. She'd picked up on the sign for home.
Home, she found herself saying now, don't worry, we're

going home soon. Found her hands making the sign for
home, fingers meeting to form a steeple.

Tycho swung over the starboard side and sloshed to
shore, didn't mind that water poured into his boots
soaking socks and chilling toes. He made it up the rocks
and slipped onto the dock sideways. Pulled off his
goggles and replaced them with the glasses he
unsnapped from his belt. Grinning. Winking. Draped
an arm around Ilana and bent over the stretcher too.
'You'll be fine, gorgeous, off we go. Touch of
exposure.' On the way to the ambulance he was
chuckling, saying thanks to Venus, thanks to Mars,
merci to the sun, *muchas gracias a la luna.*

Sarge was a top-heavy rooster. Spray streaming
down his face, his chest, he balanced on both feet in
the boat and crowed.

'Well,' said Dorey, 'they pay money too.'

Sarge laughed. He dropped the cheque on a fold of
sheet covering her lap. 'You've got it. Beer money and
a good time thrown in, what more do you want?' All
that fun for the prize offered by this brewery. Sponsor
spilling some bucks into a few laps like malt beer
dribbling from a keg tap, advertising a product none of
the competitors used.

She didn't bother to look. Leaning her head back
on the white-cased pillows, she shuddered a little.
Painkillers couldn't kill all the spasms, they'd have to
wear themselves out overnight. Her eyes stayed open,
though, weary, a little dazed, glowing tip of pride
edging through the artificial tranquillity.

Oh, Please . . .

Oh, please—
Let me be in your team,
Let mine be the name that you pick,
Don't leave me to mope at the edge of the field,
Resenting each jump and each kick;

I promise, I'll run like the wind,
I'll twist and I'll turn and I'll pass,
I'll dazzle defenders with sparkle and speed,
You won't see my boots touch the grass;

Or maybe, I'll play at the back,
As solid and strong as a wall,
Frustrating all forwards who dare to attempt
The slightest approach with the ball;

But—
Each time they play, it's the same,
I'm left on the line, in the cold,
They never allow me to join in the game,
They always say,
'Gran, you're too old!'

Rowena Sommerville

The Match of Death

JAMES RIORDAN

We weren't the best team in the land. Last season we'd come third in the league and reached the Cup semi-finals, losing to Moscow Spartak. Not that I made much of a contribution from the youth team. Still, our coach Ivan Danko always forecast a great future for me:

'Son, you'll make a nifty centre forward one day!'

One day . . .

What day?

The year was 1941. War in Europe had been raging for a couple of years. But Hitler hadn't invaded us. You see, we had a pact: don't fight us and we won't fight you. Surely he'd honour that.

But Hitler didn't believe in fair play. He didn't play to the ref's whistle. Football obviously wasn't his game.

On the night of 21 June 1941 his army crossed our frontier. The Germans were coming. In tanks and planes and black death squads. They mowed down everything in their path.

Soon they were at the gates of Kiev. From our flat on Kreshchanka I watched the tanks rumble through

the city—ugly monsters with sinister black crosses on the sides. I hid behind the curtains, while Mum pulled me away.

'Igor, don't even look at Germans—they're vermin, a plague of rats. That's what your dad says.'

Dad had joined the Red Army with my two elder brothers a year back; they'd been holding the line before Kiev. Ahead was the foe, behind were their loved ones. Goodness knows where they were now.

After Kiev's surrender, German signs and swastikas went up on every highway, and helmeted soldiers strutted through the cobblestone streets. Out of the woodwork appeared our own creepy-crawlies, Ukrainians who greeted the Nazis as liberators, who hated Jews and communists, who offered to collaborate.

One such weasel appeared at our door one day. I knew him slightly—Alex Goncharenko, half German. I'd played football with him in the Juniors. Funny that: he was a coward even then, afraid of a hard tackle, yet elbowed you in the face when the ref's back was turned.

Anyway, this fellow barges his way in and says, 'You're to report to the stadium at nine sharp tomorrow! Bring your kit.'

That was all. I was puzzled. The league was wound up at the end of the 1940 season, though we'd played a few friendlies after that—even one against a German side from Dresden. It was supposed to cement German-Soviet relations.

We lost 3–1, though we won the vodka-drinking contest afterwards . . .

Next day I took the tram down to the football ground, arriving just before nine. A German soldier

checked my passport and ticked off the name 'Igor Grechko' on his list.

Most of our youth team was already in the changing room, ranged along the wall, staring sullenly at the concrete floor. I was pleased to see my best mate Abram Feldman and I shoved in alongside him. A few of the first team and reserves drifted in. Last to arrive was the Club Coach Ivan Danko and his assistant Oles Ogapov.

Close behind them came a grim-faced German officer and two local 'helpers'. One was the weasel Goncharenko.

With so many bodies crammed into the room, the air was soon thick with cigarette smoke and sweat. It was Danko who addressed us, nervily.

'Sit yourselves down wherever you can, lads. We've been asked to hold a training session for our guests.'

He spoke the word 'guests' like you say 'lovely weather for the time of year' when it's raining cats and dogs. Clearly, as an old-time communist, he hated the Nazis; but somehow he had to protect his 'boys'.

'We'll split into firsts and seconds,' he said.

He started picking the teams.

I was in the seconds, pulling on a light blue shirt with our famous 'D' for Dinamo on the pocket, and white shorts; the firsts were in the customary white shirts and black shorts.

The German kept silent, though the shifty-eyed weasel was whispering in his ear, presumably translating and commenting on each player. Just as we were changing into our kit, the German came over to where I was sitting.

'You, Jew!' he barked. 'Stay put!'

He was pointing a black-gloved hand at Abram.

A deathly quiet descended. Abram was ours, one of our best young players. Until then no one had given any thought to him being Jewish. We had Tatars, Russians, Jews, Ukrainians, even a German in our pre-war squad. But nobody ever saw them as being anything but part of the team.

Coach's rasping voice cut through the silence.

'He plays or no one plays!'

The German glared at Danko, yet stood aside as Abram and I left the changing room together.

Once out on the pitch in the warmth of late August, we breathed in the fresh smell of grass and bindweed. For a while we could forget the war; we were playing the game we loved.

The stone terraces rang hollowly to our shouts, the goalposts were netless, the blue sky was dotted with grey barrage balloons and dark warplanes. A gaggle of old women with clumps of birch sticks were sweeping the track around the pitch.

We sprinted and leapt in the air, scored goals galore, ran off our nervous energy and puffed and beamed through honest sweat. Abram, our left half, set me up for two goals and I returned the compliment. It was nice to beat our seniors for a change.

After an hour or so Coach blew his whistle and we all trooped off. The showers had no hot water, just a dribble of cold, brackish liquid that hardly wet our heads. We didn't mind.

'Well done, you Constables,' yelled Danko.

Dinamo was known to its fans as 'the Constables'—because the Club was run by the security police.

'Same time tomorrow, comrades, on the dot,' shouted Coach. 'We've a big match on Sunday.'

We wondered what he meant. What 'big match'? Who were we playing?

'Win For Me!'

I went home on the tram with Abram who lived just round the corner, on Lenin Avenue.

'Come and have a glass of tea,' he said. 'I want you to meet someone.'

Like mine, Abram's dad was away in the army. But the cramped flat was full to bursting with little children. There was a sad-eyed skinny lad huddled in the corner; I'd not seen him before. Despite the summer heat, he was shivering.

'This is David,' said Abram. 'He's my cousin; he escaped from Rovno. Go on, tell him, David.'

Words tumbled from the skinny youth like coins from a fairground machine.

'They came for us in the night . . . beat us with rifles, shot the old and sick, even little kids, took us to a football field on the edge of town; then they lined us up and opened fire.

'Mum fell on top of me, covering me with her body. When it was dark I crawled out. Everyone was dead; it was awful.'

He broke down and sobbed as Abram's mother put one arm round him, handing me my tea with the other.

I didn't understand.

'Were you sheltering partisans?' I asked. 'Was it revenge for killing a German? Why should they do that?'

'Because we're Jews,' said Mrs Feldman quietly.

As I walked home, my head was full of unanswered questions. But all my doubts evaporated late that evening. Shouts, groans, curses and the noise of tramping feet rose from the street five storeys below. As I rushed to the window, I saw an astonishing sight. Coming down the road was a pitiful column of ragged

women, children, and old men. They were flanked by
soldiers, bellowing and hitting stragglers with their rifle
butts.

For one ridiculous moment it reminded me of a
crowd of rival football fans being escorted away after a
match. But fans weren't tiny tots in nighties, women
with streaming hair, old men on crutches, trying to
walk with dignity—and soldiers treating people like
animals.

Football fans got more respect.

We turned out the lights so as not to be seen. The
column was now passing beneath our block and, all at
once, I heard someone call my name.

'Igor, win for me!'

I couldn't see him in the gloom, but I knew the
voice.

Win what? The war? I wasn't sure what he meant.

My head was still swimming with the previous
night's events when I reported at the stadium next
morning. At least half a dozen faces were missing
including Abram's. But Coach's calm, if ashen, face
gave us comfort. No one dared mention our missing
team-mates.

'Right, lads, listen carefully. I don't care who hears
since my days are numbered. But I *do* care about you.
You are *my* players, *my* team, *my* family. We've a big
match on Sunday, the day after tomorrow.'

We all looked at each other, hoping we'd be in the
team. Then came the bombshell.

'We're playing a crack Gestapo team from Germany.
The Nazis want to demonstrate their superiority. So the
idea, dear friends, is for us to lose. If not . . .'

He drew a finger across his throat.

'Win and die, lose and survive . . .' he muttered,
half to himself. 'It's a Game of Death.'

We couldn't believe it. Could football be a matter of life and death? For the first time I hoped I wouldn't make the team. And I wasn't disappointed. When the team list went up on the door after training, my name wasn't on it.

Below the team, in small scrawled letters, however, were the names of two subs: Grigorienko and Grechko.

Coach explained, 'The Germans want to allow two subs—maybe they fear we'll break their legs!'

Would my big moment come?

The Match

That day posters went up all over the city.

GERMANY v. KIEV DINAMO
2 p.m. Sunday Dinamo Stadium
Entrance free

They need not have worried. Even those who detested football would have given their back teeth to see their side thrash the Germans. Little did the fans know we were going to lose.

'Best of luck, comrades,' said Coach before we took the field. 'I won't see you again—I've served my purpose. Don't let me down: play fairly. And remember: we may not win this battle, but we'll win the war.'

He hugged each of us in turn, tears streaming down his flushed cheeks.

Our captain led us out in our changed strip of blue shirts and white shorts—the Gestapo team wore Germany's black and white colours.

As the German referee walked ahead of both sides

on to the pitch, the roar that greeted us lifted our spirits. For the first time that day, it stirred feelings of pride for my country.

I could feel shame later.

For the moment I savoured the sheer joy of seeing and hearing those fifty thousand Kiev fans shouting, '*DI - NA - MO! DI - NA - MO!*'

The thirteen players in each squad lined up in the centre for the national anthems. First came '*Deutschland über Alles*', which was met in almost total silence. Then, as massed voices got ready to sing the Soviet national anthem, over the loudspeaker came the strains of the pre-war Ukrainian hymn 'The Great Gates of Kiev'.

After a brief moment of surprise, the music was drowned out by full-throated voices belting out our proper anthem:

'So, Comrades, come rally, and the last fight will we face . . .'

There was nothing the Germans could do about it, even though the track was ringed by soldiers pointing their guns at the crowd.

The game kicked off.

I watched from the bench, kicking every ball, making every tackle, heading every cross. Naturally, we were slow on the turn, half-hearted in attack, unwilling to chase and harry. By half-time the Germans were 2–0 up, and the crowd was silent, crushed, unable to comprehend. Now and again, a bold fan whistled disappointment.

There was no Coach in the changing room. Ivan Danko had already been led away to the nearby barracks.

The second half went much like the first, and the fans showed their disgust. No longer did they get

behind us, urging us on. Now they were on our backs, telling us what they thought of our efforts.

Midway through the half, our captain limped to the touchline and said, 'Igor, get on and do your best. I'm crocked. I don't care if they shoot me. We can't let our fans down. Better die in hope than live in shame.'

Few of the fans could have heard of me. Yet my appearance on the field was greeted as if I was Dinamo's secret weapon. The game had halted for attention to a German hurt in the tackle with our captain. During the stoppage, our team gathered in our goalmouth, and I related the captain's words.

'We can't let the fans down.'

You only had to look at those haggard, hopeful faces in the crowd to realize what defeat would mean. On the other hand, if we were to win . . .

'Better die in hope than live in shame!'

'Right!' exclaimed Nestor, our goalie, spitting on the ground. 'If any of you cowards want to lose, take my jersey and I'll play out. At least I'll break a few legs before they break me.'

We smiled. No one took up his offer. Coach had ordered us to play fairly. But our mood had changed. When the match restarted we threw ourselves into the game, chased every ball and tackled like terriers. The Germans must have wondered what hit them.

Within five minutes we scored—to the delight of our fans. Fifteen minutes remained for us to draw level. The crowd willed us on, chanted, sang, shouted, swore at the Germans—Thank God the Germans didn't understand Ukrainian!

I hit the post with one pile-driver, headed against the bar when I should have scored, and then shot hopefully from a long way out. As luck would have it,

the ball caught the heel of their centre half and was
deflected into the corner of the net.

2–2.

The crowd went wild.

My first thought was of Coach. Could he hear the
cheering from his cell? I'm sure he could!

With one minute to go the game seemed all over—
and our lives were saved. The referee blew his whistle as
Nestor was challenged roughly in catching the ball. To
everyone's astonishment, the ref was pointing to the
spot. Penalty!

Even our opponents seemed embarrassed at this
blatant bias.

Amid a cascade of whistles, their captain cooly aimed
hard and low for the corner. Yet Nestor took off as if
he had springs in his heels, caught the ball and, in one
movement, threw it upfield to me.

With no one for support, I raced forward on my own.
Three defenders stood between me and the goal. I
tapped the ball through one man's legs and tore down
the right wing, drawing the second defender. Then I cut
inside to take on the other. As they converged in a
sandwich from either side, I drew back the ball with my
foot, flicked it up and over the defenders, then nipped in
between them.

My speed took me through the tackle as they crashed
into each other. That left me one-on-one with the
goalie.

For a split second I lost my nerve. Then, all at once,
Abram's words flashed through my brain: 'Win for me!'

'I will, Abram, I will.'

And I did. The ball flew into the top corner of the
net, past the goalkeeper's despairing dive.

It all happened so fast the German referee hadn't
had time to blow his whistle for full time. Now he was

standing stock still, uncertain what to do. It was only when the German captain placed the ball on the white centre spot that he gave the goal.

The fans danced and sang and cheered as if we had won the war. In a way we had. The Match of Death had turned into the Match of Life for the thousands . . . and the millions.

We could win. We did win. We will win.

Postscript

I'm writing these words from my cell. I'm not afraid to die. I'd do it all over again just to see the happiness on the faces of those fans.

Funny old game, isn't it? Who was it said: 'Football's not a matter of life or death, it's more important than that'?

Playing Pool

We all know
what we're talking about.

The silver is on the table.
The triangle of coloured spheres
will break.

Me or him.
He'll never live it down
if I win.

That's why I'm ambitious and hot
wanting to beat him
black, purple, and blue,
playing pool like a boy
with my eyes down
in the low shabby spotlight
of a yellow room.

Me or him.

The male chorus
gurgling on Guinness
hangs from the ceiling.

Balls roll, like the eyes
peering at my arse
as I bend and squint,
arch over backwards
with professional
amateur dramatics.

And pocket mouths
close and twist
as we click on
desperately.

Me or him.

The last ball hangs like smoke,
snookered, caught in its blind trap.

And how they love me when I lose.
They love me when I lose.

Julia Darling

Hotshot

NANCY BOUTILIER

A five-foot-eight-inch fifth grader is probably going to
be one of the best basketball players in her school no
matter if she's girl or boy. But I happen to be a girl,
and pretty good at sticking the 'J' too, so don't go
challenging me to one-on-one, unless, of course, you
don't mind losing. And I'm not gonna play you easy on
account of what Mom calls 'ego'—especially no 'male
ego' that some boys got. I don't play easy for any
reason or anyone. It's that simple.

Most of life is simple. Too many people want to
make stuff way more difficult than it is. Like the time
school pictures came back and I was holding a pencil
behind Tony Kramer's head so it looked like the pencil
grew right out of his ear. Well, Mrs Kramer goes and
calls my teacher and then my mom and we all have to
sit down and discuss it. They all try to tell me what a
horrible thing I did, messing up the picture and all.
And I kept trying to tell them how funny it was—and
even Tony thought so too—but no one else was
laughing. So I end up feeling bad about something I

thought was fun—and I would never have done it to
someone like Laurie Strandy or Darius Silvers because
I know it would have made them feel bad. But Tony—
I knew he could take it.

Oh, well, I guess I'm supposed to be learning the
when's and where's of having fun. And what I like
most is fun on the basketball court. Shooting,
dribbling, rebounding—I can outrun and outjump
anyone in the fifth or sixth grade—anyone!

Most of the teachers gave up on trying to make me
stay on the girls' side of the hardtop. But old Miss
Monzelli, who I call Miss Von Smelly when she can't
hear me, sometimes still screeches from behind those
pointy glasses with the fake little diamonds for me to
get onto the hopscotch side of the blacktop. She says I
can't play with the boys because it ain't ladylike. She
says I might get hurt. She also says that saying *ain't*
ain't ladylike neither, so I do it just to remind her
who's boss. We'll see who's going to get hurt.

Truth is, no boy ever hurt me more than I hurt
him. Besides, I've had stitches four different times, and
not once have I even cried at the blood or the needles.
Broke a bundle of bones, too—three fingers, my wrist,
both collarbones, and my left ankle—seven altogether.

That's how I learned that basketball is in me—it's in
my bones. Every time I've been sidelined, I don't mind
missing out on a football game, or the roller coaster at
the carnival, but not being able to play hoops sets my
skin crawling. I know it's in my blood too because my
dad is six-foot-four and played in college. He still plays
at the Y, and I get to shoot around at halftime of his
games. All the referees there like me. Sure, they have to
show off, spinning the ball on their fingers or throwing
it to me behind the back, but they all like me. I figure
they are jealous of the guys like Dad who get to strut

their stuff while they only get to run up and down the court blowing whistles and ticking everyone off.

But at halftime, the refs rebound for me and call me Hotshot.

I'm telling you all this so you can see how some things are born in a girl, even though most people seem to think they're reserved only for boys. And don't go calling me tomboy unless you can give account of what it means. I'm a girl who can throw a football further and with a better spiral than anyone at Maple Street School, except for Greg Merrit, who is my best friend, and Mr Leon, the gym teacher. I don't mind that Greg can throw further than me because he's real good and that's just that. I can respect that. Besides, I'm a better free throw shooter than he is, so really, we're even. But don't go saying that I throw like a boy any quicker than you'd say that Greg throws like a girl, which he does, because he throws like me, and I'm a girl. There's nothing tomboy about it. I'm a girl and I can play a wizard game of Horse, I'm unbeatable at Round the World, I hold my own in 21, and you'll want me on your side if we're playing five-on-a-side pickup. I told you, it's that simple.

And I'm not good just because I'm tall. My dad told me not to be worried about being a six-foot girl because he says if any girl is going to dunk in high school it's going to be me. Mom says I slouch too much. I don't think I slouch at all. I just lean kind of forward when I walk and bounce on my toes so I can feel my hightops hugging my ankles. Air Hotshot! I hit the ground and my treads spring me right back up on my toes. I can see that it scares the boys a bit when I stride out onto the court bouncing like I'm the best thing since the hook shot in my black leather Cons. I'll take hightops over high heels any day!

Anyhow, what I'm trying to tell you about is my problem with Miss Monzelli. She's my Social Studies teacher who seems to think she got hired by the school solely to mess with my life. She tries to make me play only with the other girls at recess, and I told her I don't have anything against girls, but I like playing basketball, and it's the boys who play basketball. She says I'm not learning to be a lady if I don't play with girls and held me after school to point out that if I dress like the boys and talk like the boys, I'll find myself in trouble. It seemed to me that the only trouble I was in was with her, but I didn't think I'd score points by telling her so. Instead, I asked her if it was bad for me to be like the boys, why wasn't it bad for the boys to be like boys. After all, I didn't see her making no fuss about what they were wearing or playing.

Miss Monzelli got all red in the face so that her cheeks and neck matched the fire-engine-red lipstick she wears. She chewed me out for being fresh, and then insisted that the boys are supposed to act like boys because they are boys. It didn't make sense to me, so I didn't listen to most of what she was saying until I caught on that she had phoned my mom to say that I was supposed to wear dresses to school unless we were scheduled for gym class. Well, we only have gym twice a week, so Miss Von Smelly was saying that I had to wear a dress every Monday, Wednesday, and Friday! Now, I don't even like wearing dresses when I go to see my grandmother in the city, but that's the deal. And even then I don't like it, but my grandmother does. Gram is worth pleasing for the way she lets me climb on through the attic to the roof. Gram keeps a treasure chest for me in the closet and takes me to the zoo. Her oatmeal cookies are the best on this planet, and I get to lick the

batter from the bowl. She even sewed me a pair of
pyjamas with tiger stripes and a long tail stuffed with
nylon stockings. For Gram I will wear a dress.

Mom gave up with me and dresses when I was in
the third grade. That's when we agreed that I wouldn't
fight over wearing a dress for Sunday mass or for visits
to Gram. If I didn't put up a stink on those occasions,
I wouldn't have to wear dresses the rest of the whole
year. At Gram's house and God's house, it makes Mom
happy if I wear a dress, but no way am I wearing no
dress for no old Miss Von Smelly—not even if she
could bake oatmeal cookies like Gram's. Mom's only
other rule was 'No hightop sneakers when wearing a
dress!' I don't much mind that rule, because hightops
just don't look right when you got a skirt flapping
around your thighs.

Mom lets me wear low-cut sneakers with my knee
socks, so I can still run around, because I wear shorts
underneath. I just don't like the idea that when I
sprint, jump, fall, or wrestle the whole world has a
front-row seat to my underwear. And if I wear a dress
to school, I have to put up with all Miss Von Smelly's
stupid comments to us girls to sit with our knees locked
together so our legs get all sore and cramped from
trying to keep ourselves all shut up tight under our
desks, as if it isn't easier to just tell the boys they got
no business looking up our skirts in the first place.

I've never seen Miss Von Smelly in pants, and I feel
like telling her how much happier she'd be if she didn't
have to pay so much worrytime making sure her
underwear ain't on display when she bends over, or
reaches up high, or just stands in the wind. She wears
all these silly shoes that make her look like a Barbie
doll when she walks—stiff-kneed and pointy-toed,
scuttering along.

I don't understand Miss Monzelli any better than she understands me, but I don't go telling her that she should be wearing hightop sneakers and jeans, so where does she get off calling my mom to say that I have to dress like her? That's all I want to know.

So anyway, I go home, and at dinner, Mom tells Dad about Miss Monzelli's phone call, and I just about choke on a tomato when Dad says 'If that's what the teacher says, I suppose Angela will just have to put up with the rule.'

'But, Dad, Miss Monzelli is such a witch. She's just making me wear dresses because she knows how much I hate it! She's out to get me!'

'Now, Tiger,' Dad calls me 'Tiger' when we horse around or when he wants me to think that he's on my side, but he's really not. 'I'm sure Miss Monzelli is not out to get you. She is your teacher, and she knows what is best for you and for the school.'

'I'm not wearing dresses three times a week!'

'Honey,' Mom calls me that when I start getting stubborn, and I can tell it's going to be two against one, three against one if you count Miss Monzelli. 'I've let you take responsibility for your wardrobe this year, but maybe it's time that we take another look at what is appropriate attire for a young lady in your school. What do the other girls wear?'

'Mom,' I could hear the whine in my voice, which meant that I knew reasoning wouldn't really work, 'the other girls in my school play hopscotch at recess, and go to the corner store for Doritos and Coke after school. They don't play basketball or football or even climb on the jungle gym.'

'Well, you could come home and change into your play clothes after school if you wanted to . . . '

'Aww, come on, Mom, I'd never get in the game if I

came home while the kids were choosing up teams. Dad . . . ' I looked hopefully to my father for support, but he was staying out of this argument for as long as possible.

'Angela,' my father said with a mix of sympathy and hesitation in his voice, 'your teacher seems to think . . . '

'Dad, my teacher is a witch who waddles around in high heels and can't even hold a football in one hand. She picks it up at arm's length with two hands, like it's a piece of corn on the cob, too hot to bring within three feet of her body.'

'Now, that's no way to talk about your teacher.'

'Then there's no way she should talk about me as if I have no right to dress as I please.'

Both my parents seemed to be defending Miss Monzelli only because she was my teacher, but I could tell that words were not going to convince them of what a jerk Miss Monzelli was being. So I sat quiet, hoping they would just forget about it, and life would go on as usual as I trotted off to school in my hightops and jeans the next morning. Besides, I didn't even own enough dresses to get through a week without repeating, unless I wore the satin dress I had from being the flower girl at my cousin's wedding. That dress puffed out so that I looked like a piece of Double Bubble Chewing Gum wrapped up and twisted in bows at both ends. No way was I stepping out of the house in that thing!

My other two dresses had both been made by Gram. My favourite was yellow with purple and white stripes down the side and a big number 32 on the front. Gram made it special to look like Magic Johnson's Lakers uniform. For a dress, it's pretty neat, but it's still a dress. None of the other dresses I own fit me because I've been growing too fast for my clothes to keep up

with me. The only reason the gum-wrapper dress fits is because an older cousin was supposed to be the flower girl, but she got some mono-disease right before the wedding, and I had to take her place. The dress was too big in the first place.

So Mom and Dad go on as if this conversation is over. I dig into my fish stick as if there's something special about fish sticks, which there definitely is not. I hear my fork scratching my plate, Mom's bracelets knocking against each other, and Dad's jaw cracking the way that it does when he chews. In our family, that's a silent dinner table.

When Mom gets up to clear the table, I leap up to help because I don't want anyone pointing out how much I hate all this housework stuff as if it's because I don't wear dresses often enough. Besides, it helps change the tone of everything for dessert, and we have forgotten the whole conversation enough so that Dad pulls out the weekend football pool that he gets at work. It's the first round of the play-offs, and I'm still hopeful enough to believe that I can bet on the Patriots to make it to the Super Bowl. Dad says that his football sense overrules his loyalty to the home team, so he plays his card differently than I play mine. We argue a bit about whether or not the Patriots can get their ground game going, and then we turn our attention to the chocolate pudding Mom puts in front of us. The silence is broken, and when I go to bed I feel sure no one will notice what I wear to school in the morning.

'Do you have Phys Ed today?' Mom asks as I throw my backpack full of books on the kitchen floor by the backdoor.

'Umm, no. Why?' I pretend innocence and ignorance of Miss Monzelli's mandate.

'Well, because, we agreed that you'd save your jeans for gym days.' Mom's trying to be as forgetful of the argument as I am.

'We agreed that I could wear whatever I wanted except for church and for Gram. We never agreed to anything about wearing dresses to school. Miss Von Smelly just poked her nose into something that is not her business.' Since this was not one of those times when giving in for the sake of keeping Mom happy was worth it, I made sure not to say *ain't*. I didn't want her to have any dirt on me in any way. Otherwise, I'd be stuck for good. I hoped she'd see this as one of those times when giving in for the sake of keeping *me* happy would be worth *her* while.

It wasn't.

'Angie, the school has its expectations and standards, and you have to . . . '

'Mom, it's not the school. It's Miss Monzelli! And she's an old witch anyway. Why listen to her?'

Dad walked in and silence returned.

I grew impatient and started pleading. 'Mom, watch. No one will say anything's wrong if you just let me keep doing what I'm doing.'

'Uh-oh, dresses again, huh? Tiger, why don't you just put on a dress, go to school, and do whatever it is you always do?' offered Dad, trying to be helpful and healing to the conversation.

'Daaaddddd,' I whined, hoping the tone said more than the word itself.

'Tiger, no one is asking you to change yourself. Nobody is going to stop you from being who you are. It's only your clothes we're asking you to change.'

'Well, if it's only clothes, then why is everyone else making such a gigantic deal about what I wear?'

For a moment I grew hopeful when my dad had no answer for me, but then Mom filled the pause. 'Because your teacher thinks you ought to dress up a bit more—like the other girls.'

'Exactly,' seconded Dad. 'So why don't you run back into your room, slip those clothes into your backpack for after school, and put on a dress for classes?'

It was more of a commandment than a question, and I knew I wasn't going to get out of the house in my jeans. So I just glared at Dad a bit, then glared even harder at Mom, and stormed back to my room.

I had tried to be honest with my parents, but my honest opinions had gotten me nowhere. I didn't really want to cut school, although that option did come to mind. I figured I could change my clothes as soon as I got around the corner from the house. So, I put on the dress I hated most, the candy-wrapper one from Rico's wedding. It looked really stupid with my sneakers, and I felt like irking my folks because they were siding with Miss Von Smelly. I wore one tube sock with black and orange stripes and one with green and blue stripes, all of which completely clashed with the yellow and red of the dress.

I stomped my way back into the kitchen, no longer hungry for breakfast. I stood in the doorway as defiantly as possible with legs spread wide and arms folded across my chest. Mom and Dad looked at each other, unimpressed by me, and pleased as punch they'd won the argument. I stuffed my jeans and a T-shirt into my backpack as Dad had suggested, but I guess he must've been onto my plan to change before I reached the schoolyard because he offered to drive me to school.

Next thing I know, Dad's dropping me off in the school parking lot, and I'm facing a blacktop filled with my friends who have never even seen me in a dress, let alone in a flower girl gown, and I can't believe it. I'm angry as can be at Mom, Dad, Miss Monzelli, and any kid who dares to look at me. I turn to get back into the car, and when Dad innocently waves 'So long, Tiger. See you tonight,' I can't believe he's humiliating me this way. I see a few kids pointing towards me, laughing, and I want to punch them all. I don't know where to begin swinging, so I run inside to the girls' room, leap into the second stall, lock the door, and stand up on the seat so that no one can find me.

As I'm catching my breath, I discover that I left my backpack in the car.

Everybody has already seen me and I'm weighing my options while perched atop the toilet. Then I hear the bathroom door squeak open. By the clicking of tiny footsteps echoing across the tile, I know Miss Monzelli has stalked me down.

'Hello? Is anyone in here? Hello? Angela? Angela?'

I say nothing, but I think of how stupid I'll feel if she finds me hiding in the stall. I know she knows I'm in here. I quickly and quietly slide my feet down so that it looks like I'm sitting on the toilet, and I drop my underpants down around my ankles. 'Yes, Miss Monzelli,' in the sweetest voice I can put together. 'I'm just, well, ya know, doing what I have to do.'

'Oh, Angela, it's you,' she says, as if she's surprised I'm here. 'I saw someone sneak in, and you know you shouldn't leave the playground without permission. Unless of course it's an emergency. I suppose it's all right this one time if Nature caught you by surprise.' She's trying to make me feel better, but it sure as cinnamon ain't working.

'By the way, I thought you looked very pretty when I saw your father drop you off.'

That was the final straw. I wanted to scream, punch, or puke at her. She sounded so smug in her triumph, like those TV preachers who have saved some stupid sinner from the clutches of the devil. But fighting Miss Von Smelly would be no solution. It would only help prove to her that I behaved unladylike. So I said nothing, and she filled the silence by explaining that she was going back out before the bell rang to line everyone up for homeroom. Again, the bathroom door squeaked and the echoing heel clicks out of the door and down the hallway.

I hated the thought of being made a fool of by Miss Monzelli's dumb rules. I needed a way to make her own rules work for me rather than against me. So I sat for a bit, realizing I might as well pee while I was on the toilet. After finishing my piss, I stood and reached to pull my underwear back up. As I turned to flush, a comic vision flashed through my head. I quickly dropped my underwear back to my ankles and stepped out of one leg hole. With my other leg, I kicked it up into the air, then with one arm I reached out to first catch and then slam dunk my underwear into the toilet bowl. A quick kick to the metal bar flushed it all away. No more underwear!

Miss Monzelli could gloat all she wanted over her little victory because I knew I'd have the last laugh. I wasn't thrilled about the razzing I'd have to put up with in the meantime, but it would all be worthwhile.

I returned to the blacktop where everyone was lining up silent and military. Eyes flashed my way, and an occasional head turned, but always at the risk of Miss Monzelli taking away recess period for headturners to

practise standing at attention. I always wondered what
it was we were supposed to pay attention to.

I held my head high and looked at no one. I had a
secret that would teach Miss Monzelli not to mess with
my life or my wardrobe so I figured I didn't have to deal
with any kid's questions or stares. I just strutted to my
place in the back of the line, glad that my last name was
Vickery so I was at the end of the alphabetical order that
Miss Monzelli organizes her life by. I glared down at
Eric Tydings who stood in front of me every time we
lined up for anything. He turned with a giggle held under
his breath, and I answered his jeering. 'If you don't turn
around and get rid of that jackass grin, I'm gonna make
your teeth permanent fixtures in your stomach.'

Eric quickly turned back to the front, and it was a
good thing for him, because the line was filing into the
school, and Miss Monzelli for sure would have slapped
him with some detention time for not paying attention.
And no way was she going to blame me for his mischief
today. After all, I was wearing a dress, and in Miss
Monzelli's book, girls in dresses act ladylike and stay
out of trouble.

I spoke to no one all morning except to answer
questions with 'yes' or 'no', because I had nothing
much I wanted to say to anyone. We had lots of stuff
to do, including a worksheet of word problems, some
reading about astronauts, and a spelling test. I
pretended not to notice all the attention I was
getting—but inside I wasn't missing a single sidelook
or whisper. All the while I sat real careful not to let on
that I wore nothing beneath my dress. I wanted to be
sure that Miss Monzelli could not get word that I had
no underwear on. I was determined that the whole
school should see for themselves all at the same time,
so I waited patiently for morning recess.

The recess bell finally rang at 10:30 just as I was completing an essay about my favourite animal. I had written all that I could think of writing about kangaroos about five minutes earlier, but I added one final sentence to my essay before putting up my pencil and folding my hands together on my desk top the way Miss Monzelli insists we all sit before she will consider allowing us to line up for recess. I wrote, 'Kangaroos prove God has a sense of humour because the only reason kangaroos exist is to jump around and have fun.'

I signed my essay the way I always do at the end. Miss Monzelli hates it because she wants my name squished up at the top right corner of the page, neatly printed with her name and the date. She insists we use the 'proper heading' on our work, so I do that, but I also let loose in big script letters at the end 'by Angela Vickery' like a painter signing a masterpiece.

'All right, children. You may line up quietly in alphabetical order if you would like to go outside for recess.' Of course everyone wanted to go out for recess, but Miss Monzelli always made it sound like an option and an invitation all at the same time that it was really, deep down, just another Von Smelly command.

We lined up, with me in the back again, and filed silently down the corridor to the double doors that lead to the playground. Once outside we were allowed to break file, and we scattered ourselves across the blacktop. Kevin Marino was close on my heels asking, 'Hey, Angela. What's with the dress?' and I was answering only with an all-out sprint to the basketball court. Tyrone Freeman had the ball, and he was starting a game of 21 rather than choosing up sides for full court. Recess was too short for a game, and 21 gave everyone a chance to play because it's one big half-court game that leaves everyone against everyone

scrapping to make a basket. You just have to keep track of your own score, and it's you against everyone any time you get the ball.

So I threw out my elbows the way I always did and made space for myself in the middle of the crowd huddled below the basket. The boys knew me well enough to tell from the scowl on my face that questions or jokes were completely out of order, so we all just settled in to play basketball. When Tyrone missed an outside shot, the rebound went off my fingers, and Stu Jackster came up with the ball. He cleared the ball out past the foul line, and I went out with him to play defence. He drove to my left, but his leg caught my knee, and we both went to the pavement. I landed sitting flat on my fanny with Stu sprawling across my legs. My dress was all in place, and Stu spit at the pavement beside me as he extended a hand to help me up. Meanwhile, the ball had gotten loose, and Greg Merrit had scored on a jump shot.

Greg got to take the ball up top because it's 'make it—take it' where you get the ball back after you score a hoop. As Greg went to take a shot from the top of the key, I went back under to rebound. Sure enough, I came up with the ball, and put it straight up for a point of my own. It was my ball, at the top, and I took the ball left, spun around back to the right, and after two dribbles, I put the ball up and off the backboard for another basket.

My ball again. This time Tyrone decides to play me close, and as I move to spin past him, he gets help on the double team from Greg Merrit. BANG! Greg and I collide, and this time I'm on my back with my hightop sneakers looking down at me. Tyrone screams, 'She's got no underwear on!' and they're all laughing hysterically. I clench my teeth almost as tightly as my

fists and hiss out at them with squinted eyes, 'Miss
Monzelli says I gotta wear a dress. Man, I'm wearing a
dress, aren't I? You laugh at her, not at me, Tyrone
Freeman. If any of you wanna laugh at me, you gonna
have all your faces rearranged!'

Tyrone backed down on account we're friends, but
Doug McDermott wasn't so smart. He starts chanting,
'I see London. I see France. Angela got no
underpants.' Once Doug gets going, everyone joins
him, and I go right for his throat. He lands a half-
punch the side of my head, and I throw one he ducks
away from. Next thing I know, we're rolling around on
the court, neither one of us landing any punches, but
my dress is caught up high and my naked butt must be
mooning the whole world just as Miss Monzelli arrives
at the fight. Her voice is an extra two octaves higher
than usual when I hear her scream, 'Angela Vickery,
stop it! Stop this instant. Stop!'

Of course, I'm not stopping. I'm barely listening,
but she tells one of the kids to run and get Mr Stoller,
the school principal.

Well, lots of fussing went on about this whole scene.
The kids loved it. It was a scandal that had teachers
and the principal unsure about what to do. After all,
they had brought it on themselves. As Greg Merrit
said, 'You ask Angie to wear a dress and you gotta
expect something crazy!'

Mr Stoller lectured me a long while about fighting,
but he never said anything directly about my lack of
underwear. The school nurse gave me a whole lot of
nurselike advice about being clean and wearing the
proper undergarments. My mom and dad had a
conference that afternoon with Miss Monzelli, but
didn't say much to me about it.

The next day, when I arrived at breakfast in jeans

and a Lakers sweatshirt, Mom asked if I wanted Wheaties or Grapenuts and that was that. Even after all the dust settled, Miss Monzelli never brought up the subject of dresses or underwear.

When the weekend arrived, Mom announced that Gram had invited us to the city for the day. I ran back upstairs to my room and happily put on my Magic Johnson dress. When I returned to the kitchen for breakfast, Mom and Dad looked at me, and then at each other, relieved.

I answered their unasked question by quickly turning, bending and lifting my skirt to show them my underwear.

'Looking good, Tiger!' cheered Dad as I turned around to face my smiling parents.

'What are you waiting for? Go on, get dressed. I want to sink my teeth into Gram's oatmeal cookies while they're still warm.'

what if I become a body builder?

my body the tree
my body the jar
my body the saving grace
my body the dancing flesh
my body well-defined
my body looks mean
my body the tight belly they want
my body rippling flesh
my body carries around a tape measure
my body with barbells in the trunk of the car
my body one nice hunk of a lady
my body the prize winner
my body the object
my body deformed
my body redefined
my body in the flash of light bulbs
my body the champion
my body feel my biceps
my body the crowd ogles
my body well-oiled
my body loud smell
my body I take home
my body this strong woman
my body curls up alone
my body carries the weight of dreams

Tobey Kaplan

Calypso Cricket

MARK JEFFERSON

Fifth Test at Sabina Park,
Kingston, Jamaica

First Day

As it was his hundredth Test match, Fish Archibald
had been given the honour of leading the West Indies
out on to his home turf of Sabina Park. Charlie
Constantine and the rest of the side all hung back for
several moments as Fish walked out alone on to the
ground. The crowd gave him a rousing reception as
Jamaica paid tribute to one of her favourite sons. Fish
had a tear in his eye. He could hardly believe it was his
hundredth Test—it seemed like yesterday that he had
been making his debut over in England.

The ground had never been so busy. People were
sitting on the roofs of the stand and hanging from the
branches of trees that overlooked the ground. A local
builder had hoisted the cage of a crane behind the
pavilion and he stood in there with what must have
been two dozen of his friends. It was impossible to say

how many were watching, but Sabina Park was
bursting at the seams. Those who were not there were
crowded around TV sets at home or walking the streets
with radios clasped to their ears. Nobody was at work.
Everything else on the island had stopped for these five
very special Test match days.

Knightley and Churchill were back for England.
They were at full strength and had reverted to the side
which had served them so well in the first two Test
matches. West Indies were unchanged from the last
Test—Hurricane Hamish named in the team, but his
whereabouts still unknown.

The murmurs started as the people realized that the
West Indies were taking the field with a substitute—
Frankie Genus. The same conversation circulated the
ground.

'Hurricane not here then?'

'No. But Constantine has named him in the team.
Genus is just on to field as sub.'

'Wow. That's a risk, isn't it?'

Things started badly for the West Indies. In
Hurricane's absence Amory opened with Fish
Archibald, but Smith, delighted at the unexpected
bonus of not having to face the young fast bowler, got
away to a quick start. He was supported at the other
end by the rock solid defence of Robert Martin, who
had been a reliable foil to Smithy the Slogger
throughout the series.

Smith was playing all his shots, and Charlie
Constantine needed twenty men on the field to contain
him. Where are you, Hurricane? he thought to himself.
I hope I've not made a mistake.

Smith blazed away. The clock moved round, and the
runs flowed. Smith drove past mid-off, cut behind point,
glanced to fine leg, hooked to deep square leg, drove

through extra cover and clipped the ball off his legs through mid-wicket. His fifty came up in only an hour. There was still no sign of Hurricane Hamish. The crowd was as quiet as a full Sabina Park had ever been.

It started as a murmur, a hum that went around the ground—then there was an eerie sort of a hush. Charlie and Fish were standing together discussing the field for the next over, but the strange silence stopped their conversation. Charlie was aware that all eyes were turned towards the pavilion and he and Fish turned in time to see the lanky figure bounding down the steps.

'Here comes Hurricane Hamish,' said Charlie.

'Thank goodness,' replied Fish. 'We need him.'

It started as applause and grew to the biggest roar and cheering and general mayhem from a crowd any of the players had ever known.

Hurricane was running on to the field of play, putting on his shirt as he went. People were banging drums, whistles were being blown—there was a cacophony of joyous celebration. The calypso cricketer had arrived. He sprinted out on to the field to replace Genus, his bare feet springing across the historic Sabina Park outfield. It was great to be there.

Hurricane ran up to Charlie and Fish.

'Where have you been?' Charlie said, raising an eyebrow at the boy. 'And where did you get that bump on your head?'

Hurricane could only grin nervously.

'It's a long story, skipper.'

'A good one?'

'Oh. It's a good one, OK,' said Hurricane.

Charlie went over to Umpire Adams to confirm something. He came back and spoke to Hurricane.

'The rules say you've got to field for the same time you've been off. That's an hour—so we'll have to wait until after lunch to bowl you now. Let's hope Smith doesn't go too crazy in the meantime.'

Smith, however, continued to bat relentlessly and magnificently—and was soon into the nineties. The West Indies were relieved when the interval came.

No one was surprised when the first thing Charlie Constantine did as the players took the field after lunch was to throw the ball to Hurricane.

'You owe me a few wickets,' said Charlie, smiling now.

'I won't let you down. We haven't lost this one yet. I'll give you those wickets,' said Hurricane, 'I promise.'

He went to mark out his run. As he did so, he looked up to the place in the crowd where the girl had been—both for the trial and the Jamaica versus Trinidad game. He saw that the mystery girl was edging past people to take her seat. She turned and saw Hurricane looking up and raised her hand to him. Hurricane waved back.

He looked up at the scoreboard. 146 for 0. Smith 99 not out. Fish ambled over from mid-on. He put his arm around Hurricane's shoulder and said: 'Be fast! You can do it! Be fast! Come on, Hurricane. It's more important than ever.'

Hurricane charged in, his feet hardly seeming to touch the floor, he glided so gracefully into the wicket. His first ball was short outside the off stump. Smith flashed at it, hoping to steal the run he needed for his century, but the ball was through him too quickly and was in Alleyne's gloves before he even went through with the shot.

Andy Alleyne was standing a long way back, but he still took the ball way above his head. He tossed it to Charlie, who was at first slip, and whistled in appreciation at the sting in the palms of his hands.

'Now that *was* quick,' he said.

Hurricane returned to his mark. He felt very loose, very strong. He charged in for the next delivery. It was full and straight and faster than the previous ball. It seemed to dart under Smith's helplessly flailing bat as if it had been pre-programmed to home in on the wicket. The ball was so fast that it simply snapped middle stump in two as it bowled Smith neck and crop.

The West Indies players ran to congratulate Hurricane. Smith trudged off, upset to have missed his century, but totally astonished by the speed of that delivery. He wished Hurricane had stayed away.

The crowd were dancing around. They had started a carnival. They knew that the West Indies were on their way.

It had been quite some day. Hurricane's arrival had set the crowd alight and had given a whole new impetus to the West Indies team. As well as picking up the vital wicket of Smith, Hurricane had also bowled Bingley and had Darcy caught at first slip by Charlie Constantine. He had bowled as fast and as accurately as he could remember—finishing with 3 for 37 off 20 overs. What was more, he had raised the spirits of the other bowlers. All of them had chipped in with wickets, as England collapsed to 289 all out, only Bertram and Wentworth managing any sort of a score after the opening pair had been dismissed. If the batsmen could do their stuff tomorrow, thought Hurricane, a win was back on the cards. The series might still be theirs.

Second Day

The batsmen did not do their stuff—indeed, by the time Hurricane walked out to the wicket later on in the day, they had been reduced by England to 162 for 9.

It all started as badly as possible with ducks for both Constantine and Scorpio—West Indies were 0 for 2 at one stage. It was overcast throughout and the seam quartet of Willoughby, Wickham, Wentworth, and Darcy moved the ball around all day—both in the air and off the wicket. There were some close lbw decisions which went England's way and two crazy run-outs, which could only be put down to the nerves of the occasion getting the better of some of the West Indies players. A few of the batsmen got a decent start, but none of them had gone on to make a big score.

Hurricane's march to the crease did not exactly fill anyone with confidence. His reputation preceded him, and on the one occasion he had batted so far in these Test matches he had been bowled first ball for a duck. Willoughby stood at the end of his run, licking his lips in anticipation. Hurricane always looked so awkward in his pads and gloves and helmet, and he had to wear boots for batting, which made him somehow unbalanced.

Fish Archibald was at the non-striker's end and walked down for a word.

'Shuffle across and just try and get something on it. We need every run we can muster. Do your best.'

'I will,' said Hurricane. 'But I'm not very good at batting.'

Fish smiled. As if he didn't know.

Willoughby knew this, too, and he delivered just what was required—a fast, straight yorker. Hurricane jabbed down on it too late and was bowled for yet another golden duck. The crowd let out a disappointed

sigh and Hurricane hung his head in disappointment. West Indies all out for 162—giving England a very healthy and potentially match-winning first innings lead of 127.

Hurricane came out at the back of the line, pleased to be taking the field with the rest of the team this time. The team gathered in a huddle in the way they had become accustomed to under Charlie Constantine. He got them thinking about the job in hand.

'Hurricane,' he said. 'I want you to take the first over. I'm going to set you straight at Smith. If we can get him out early we may have a chance of getting back into this game. An early breakthrough is vital.'

Hurricane marked out his run and Fish came over from mid-off for his usual few words with him, encouraging Hurricane to really let it rip and give Smith a proper working over.

Hurricane's first ball was a no-ball, but it simply took off from just short of a length. Despite Andy Alleyne's desperate jump, it flew over the wicket-keeper's head and clattered into the sight-screen behind him for four byes. Smith stood back and twirled his bat, pretending to be unruffled, but thinking that he had never seen anyone as quick as this kid.

The next ball was legitimate, but just as fast. Smith flung his head back, flicked at it, got a thick edge and the ball flew all the way over the head of Sherwin Padmore at third man into the tenth row of the crowd for six. It had been so fast that Smith had merely helped it on its way.

Now Hurricane tried to bowl a slower one. Smith picked it, took two steps down the wicket and smashed it back over Hurricane's head for six more. The crowd

was silenced. It was an incredibly aggressive start once again from Smith—fighting fire with fire.

Fish came over to Hurricane.

'Forget about the slower ones. Just be fast.'

Hurricane nodded. More importantly, he searched once again for the familiar figure in the stand and managed to pick her out amongst the thousands of faces. The mystery girl was there.

'Be fast,' he urged himself. 'Come on. You can do it.'

The next ball was the fastest Hurricanc had ever bowled. It fired towards Smith's stomach. He jerked the bat up to protect himself but the ball smacked straight into the handle and the force flung the bat clean out of Smith's hands and on to his stumps.

Smith stood confused but Alleyne and the slips were shouting and Umpire Adams had his finger up. Smith was out hit wicket. The bat had simply been ripped from his hands by Hurricane's pace. England were 16 for 1.

Yet this was not the start of the batch of wickets the West Indies needed. For the rest of the day Martin and Ferrers dug in very effectively. Hurricane and Fish bowled well, but with no luck, and England finished the day on 66 for 1—a lead of 193, and in a strong position to win the match.

Third Day

Everything came right for Hurricane on the third day. Only one man could cope with his blistering pace. George Knightley found his best form and batted quite beautifully for a glorious century.

The rest of the English batsmen found Hurricane too hot to handle. He got Martin early on for 25, then

Ferrers for 30, Bingley for 2, Darcy for 8, Wentworth for 4, and Willoughby for 10. With Smith's wicket the day before this gave Hurricane 7 for 62—his best Test figures to date.

He bowled tirelessly, accurately and with sustained hostility—it was a rare exhibition of the art of top-class pace bowling. Charlie asked him a couple of times if he wanted a breather, but Hurricane refused to come off.

Archibald, Amory, and King also picked up a wicket each and England were all out, early on in the final session, for 272. The crowd simply rose to Hurricane as he led the team off. The boy had certainly come of age today—ten wickets in the match once again and he had carried the West Indies bowling attack.

The crowd was a knowledgeable one, though, and they were realists about the West Indies' chances. This bowling display was about as good as the West Indies could have hoped for, but it still left them with 400 to win—a very large score to make in the last innings of a Test match.

They started well enough, finishing the day on 60 for 0—Charlie Constantine looking very comfortable on 19 and Radwick Scorpio having played some lovely shots to make 39. They needed 340 more to win—and the target still looked a fair way off.

Fourth Day
The West Indies started badly in the morning, losing Scorpio immediately and then Matthews cheaply to the bowling of Willoughby. They had soon slumped to 67 for 2. The game had swung firmly England's way once again.

Yet, at the other end, Charlie Constantine was playing himself in to bat most of the day for one of the

innings of his life. He played as well as any of the thousands of Jamaicans watching could ever remember him having played, scoring runs very quickly and stroking the England bowlers all around Sabina Park. Would anyone stay with him though? The West Indies lost James for 28 and Goldman for 17.

After lunch Constantine went to his century and the West Indies were now 189 for 4. Wicket-keeper Andy Alleyne joined him and batted very purposefully and with great aggression. The game was swinging back towards the West Indies until Wentworth found Alleyne's outside edge and keeper Churchill took the catch. 281 for 5. 119 still needed. The tension in the ground was unbearable.

Constantine had only Larry King and then the tail-enders for support now, so he continued to play his shots, trying to eat into the total as quickly as possible. King supported him well before being bowled by a sharp off-spinner from Bertram for 27.

322 for 6.

Padmore came and went quickly, caught at short leg off Wickham.

333 for 7.

There were 67 needed, but only three wickets left—and one of those was Hurricane Hamish, yet to make a run in Test cricket.

The light was now coming in quickly—but by now Constantine and Amory were on top of the bowlers and putting together a very good partnership. The umpires offered the chance to come off for bad light but Charlie decided to bat on. The England team was getting edgy and Charlie felt on top of his game. The score edged upwards. 350. Then 360. Soon the West Indies were 370 for 7. Only 30 needed.

Darcy was juggling his bowlers as best he could, but

his seamers were tired. 380 came up. A total hush enveloped the crowd as victory was coming within reach.

Charlie Constantine mopped his brow and called for a drink from the dressing-room. He had a chat with Roy Amory, telling him to keep going as he was—he was doing brilliantly.

Constantine hit Wickham for two boundaries through the off side and a two through mid-wicket.

390 for 7.

Darcy tossed the ball to Bertram. Constantine pushed him through mid-off for a quickly scampered single.

391 for 7.

Amory worked Bertram past point for 3.

394 for 7.

There were six needed. Charlie surveyed the field, wondering whether to go for a big hit. The fifth ball of Bertram's over was slightly over-pitched. Constantine clipped it wide of mid-on for four.

398 for 7.

Only two more runs were needed. Bertram bowled again. The ball kept low and in the poor light Charlie could not get his bat on it in time and was hit on the pad. The whole England team shouted as one at Umpire Murray—Charlie had never heard a shout like it.

Owwwzzzaaaaaaaaaaaaaaaaaaaatttttttttttttt!

Murray took some time over his decision, deciding that it had hit in line and was going on to take leg stump. The finger went up and the crowd groaned.

Then they rose as one to cheer Charlie off the ground after the most memorable of innings. He was out for 196, just short of a double-century, but a truly great innings in the context of the whole history of the

game of cricket. No one could remember having seen anything quite like it.

398 for 8—and it was even darker now, but only two overs were left in the day.

Fish Archibald came in and successfully played out a maiden from Darcy. It was far too accurate to try to steal a run. Now there was one over left. Amory had to decide whether to play for tomorrow or to try to steal the winning two runs.

Bertram bowled a perfect line and length to Amory. He patted back the first five balls. The sixth spun viciously and bounced, took Amory on the glove and bounced up to Smith at short leg, who caught it. A gasp went round the ground.

398 for 9.

West Indies were still two runs short and with only one wicket left. England captain Darcy claimed the extra time to try to finish the game off, but in the gloom the umpires offered Fish the light and he decided to come off.

That was it for the day.

West Indies number 11 Hurricane Hamish was left sitting in the dressing-room, shaking like a leaf, but not required until the morning.

Fifth Day
'At least nobody will turn up,' said Hurricane hopefully at breakfast time.

FT looked up from his cooking.

'What do you mean?' he said quizzically.

'Well, the people aren't going to turn up just to see two runs or one wicket, are they?' said Hurricane.

FT shook his head and turned the kippers.

'I'm sorry, Hurricane, but you've got to face it. The

ground will be as packed as on the last four days. No
one's ever seen a series like it and they are not going to
miss the finale.'

Hurricane put his head in his hands. He knew FT
was right.

'Oh no,' he muttered. 'Don't they know I can't bat.'

'Everybody knows you can't bat,' said FT. 'Everyone
also hopes that somewhere, some day, you've got to get
just one run—or even two. Perhaps that day will be
today. You may not have to face any of the bowling
anyway. Two to win, Fish on strike. It could be OK.'

Hurricane groaned. Somehow he doubted it.

Hurricane walked to the ground and it reminded him of
the day he had first played for Jamaica. People saw his
lanky frame coming along the street and, before he knew
it, he was surrounded by little kids, jumping up to touch
him and wishing him luck. The message went down the
streets in front of him on the way to the ground.

'Here he comes. Here comes Hurricane Hamish—
the calypso cricketer!'

Old and young alike hung out of their windows and
shouted out to him.

'Good luck, Hurricane.'

'How about a run or two from you today.'

'Calypso, Hurricane. Calypso.'

Hurricane smiled and waved, but his nerves were
jangling.

If it were possible, Sabina Park was even fuller than
on the first four days. When Hurricane finally made it
through the hordes of people up to the dressing-room,
he looked out over the ground and took a minute to take
in the scene. Even the Jamaican Blue Mountains behind
the ground seemed to be straining towards the action—

eager for their own view of this dramatic day of cricketing history. No one could have scripted it like this—the drama was so intense that it seemed like today the eyes of the whole of the world were on Sabina Park.

Hurricane was rather late. Fish Archibald was already sitting there with his pads on. He had a towel over his head, concentrating and getting his mind on the job in hand. The other players stood around in their West Indies blazers and team uniform, unable to do anything today, other than watch Fish and Hurricane decide if the series would belong to them or to England.

Hurricane got changed and padded up. A few of the players came to sit with him, talking to him, trying to build his confidence. He would never have minded being in a position to decide a series with the ball—but not with the bat! Fish was still under his towel, meditating.

England needed one wicket to win.

West Indies needed one run to tie, two to win.

The match and the whole series hung in the balance.

The umpires and the England fielders were out there and it was time for Fish and Hurricane to go. Fish had a grim look of determination on his face. Hurricane just looked worried. To try to change his luck, he left his boots in the dressing-room, deciding to risk it barefoot. He went gingerly out towards the field of play behind Fish.

As they were walking out Hurricane heard a voice to one side of him.

'Hurricane! Hurricane, over here!'

He looked at the mass of people packed around where the players came out.

'Hurricane!' came the voice again.

Hurricane scanned the faces and squashed in between them he made out the face of the mystery girl. Some people made a gap for her and she squeezed through to stand before him. He stopped, frozen in front of her.

'Who are you?' he said.

She looked very intensely at him and she spoke in a voice that was serious, yet full of belief.

'Don't worry about that now,' she said. 'Just remember. You don't know how to hold the bat. Try the other way. Just try the other way. Left-handed.'

People were pushing to get a better view of Hurricane and the mystery girl disappeared back into the mass of people.

What did she mean?

There was a murmur from the crowd as Hurricane hesitated on the steps. All round the ground the crowd whispered to each other. What had Hurricane stopped for? Who had he been speaking to? Had he no boots on? Finally he came into view of the whole crowd as he started jogging on to the ground and caught up with Fish.

Inside the West Indian dressing-room Brian Lara turned to speak to Viv Richards.

Inside the England dressing-room Ian Botham turned to speak to Michael Atherton.

All round the ground people spoke in hushed tones to each other. They all said the same thing—uncertainty and anticipation in their words.

'Here comes Hurricane Hamish. Boots or no boots, I've never seen him make a run.'

Fish was facing for the first over. Darcy took the captain's responsibility of bowling it. He had bowled

accurately all series. If he could just keep Archibald at that end and prevent any runs, then Willoughby, their top fast bowler, could have a go at Hurricane Hamish in the next over. It was a risk, but it might just work.

Fish's plan was to play the first five balls of the over as positively as he could and to try to hit the runs. If not he would try to pinch a single off the last ball to keep the strike.

Darcy bowled the perfect defensive over. Each delivery was fired into the blockhole, he varied his pace, and it was all Fish could do to keep the six deliveries out—let alone hit the winning runs or even sneak a single off the last ball.

'Great bowling, captain,' said Willoughby, taking the ball from him at the end of the over. The England players changed ends eagerly. Now they had a chance to bowl at Hurricane Hamish and none of them had ever seen him look like making a run.

Up in the dressing-room the West Indies players all groaned. Some could not even watch.

'That's it,' someone said. 'We've lost.'

The crowd was quaking with nerves. Everyone was willing Hurricane to manage a good stroke. In their heart of hearts everyone knew that this was highly unlikely.

Fish sauntered down the wicket, pretending to be casual.

'Well this is it,' said Fish. 'It's now or never, Hurricane.'

He looked at the kid. He liked him so much—but if only he could bat a bit.

'I've never even hit a ball in Test cricket before,' said Hurricane.

'Isn't there something different you could try?' said Fish. 'Anything?'

Hurricane remembered the mystery girl's words.

'Well. I've an idea,' said Hurricane. 'I've always been told I don't know how to hold a bat. So, how about the other way?'

'What?' said Fish. 'You mean left-handed?'

'Why not?' said Hurricane. 'Anything is worth a try. Otherwise we've lost.'

Fish closed his eyes in prayer.

'Go on then,' he said. 'Try it.'

Hurricane went back to the crease, took guard and settled into the stance of a left-hander.

Darcy switched his field round in response to this. John Willoughby stood at the end of his run, concentrating. To him, this seemed like desperation from Hurricane. Just one straight one—one straight delivery and the series should be theirs.

The crowd were so quiet it seemed unreal. Everybody had almost stopped breathing.

Hurricane felt the bat in the unusual position in his hand. It felt OK, he thought.

Willoughby charged in. He bowled a quick in-swinger on a full length, aiming for Hurricane's exposed toes. It curved in towards middle stump and Willoughby started to raise his arms as he saw it heading on target for victory.

Hurricane Hamish took a giant stride towards the ball and, lunging blindly, his eyes closed, he swung the bat towards it. He felt a contact with the ball and heard the noise of leather on willow.

For an instant everything stood still. Hurricane opened his eyes and saw the ball squeeze out on the leg side between square leg and mid-wicket. He looked up and Fish was haring down the wicket towards him.

'Run, Hurricane,' he was screaming.

The whole crowd was screaming: 'RUN, HURRICANE!'

Hurricane set off. With his bare feet, he flew over the turf. He reached the bowler's end in an instant and turned. Fish was already heading back towards him at full pelt.

'Run, Hurricane. There's two here.'

The crowd was screaming and shouting.

'TWO, HURRICANE! RUN! RUN!'

Hurricane did not even look where the ball was. He ran like a madman down the wicket. Somewhere to his side he could hear the ball whistling in from the outfield. As he neared the wicket he dived, flinging himself full length and running his bat home before the ball thudded into Frank Churchill's gloves.

For a moment Hurricane lay outstretched on the turf. The world was suddenly full of noise— all he could hear was clapping and shouting and people calling his name. He could hear Fish somewhere.

'You did it, Hurricane. You did it.'

Hurricane was carried off the ground by a group of supporters. He held his bat and the souvenir stump which someone had given him above his head. The whole ground was cheering and shouting and chanting his name and Hurricane grinned the biggest grin in the history of the world.

Fish, who was also being carried along in the air on a sea of people, called over to him.

'Hey, Hurricane!'

'What?' shouted Hurricane above the din.

'I always said you didn't know how to hold a bat!'

Hurricane was laughing. The crowd was chanting.
'Calypso! Calypso! Calypso!'

The series trophy was presented to Charlie Constantine
and the Man of the Match award to Hurricane.

Hurricane stood with the two teams as he accepted
the trophy from Man of the Match adjudicator
Clive Lloyd. The West Indies team were all grinning
and patting him on the back and, despite their
disappointment, Mike Atherton, Fitzwilliam Darcy, and
the whole England squad were applauding him. Lara,
Ambrose, and Walsh were clapping and smiling, and
the two chairmen of selectors, Viv Richards and Ian
Botham, stood together and marvelled at such a climax
to one of the greatest ever Test series.

Hurricane looked out at the people crammed on to
the outfield, shouting and waving up at him. The
mystery girl was smiling and waving. He tried to shout
to her, but no one could hear anything for the noise.

Hurricane kissed the Man of the Match trophy and
raised it above his head, and Fish and Charlie hoisted
him up on to their shoulders. He looked across the sea
of smiling faces and waved in thanks to his adoring
fans.

First Dive

Shivering in the hot August sun
  I stand on the lowest diving board
watching above me the giants
fearlessly twist and knife
into their dark waters

I measure distance
in terms of
multiple whales
and weigh my eleven years
against the terrors
circulating quietly and steadily
under the surface
the eyes that stare from green rocks
at my naked feet
the hands weaving seaweed nets
to complete the ambiguity
of my needless capture
a surfeit of teeth and claws gathering
to oversee my fate

Reckless with fear
I become a wavering sigh
  a reluctant bird
lose head and hands and atmosphere
to trespass suddenly
into adult depths
bobbing up   transfigured   victorious
out of an unclaimed ocean.

Florence McNeil

The Big Catch

ERNEST HEMINGWAY

He awoke with the jerk of his right fist coming up against his face and the line burning out through his right hand. He had no feeling of his left hand but he braked all he could with his right and the line rushed out. Finally his left hand found the line and he leaned back against the line and now it burned his back and his left hand, and his left hand was taking all the strain and cutting badly. He looked back at the coils of line and they were feeding smoothly. Just then the fish jumped making a great bursting of the ocean and then a heavy fall. Then he jumped again and again and the boat was going fast although line was still racing out and the old man was raising the strain to breaking point and raising it to breaking point again and again. He had been pulled down tight on to the bow and his face was in the cut slice of dolphin and he could not move.

This is what we waited for, he thought. So now let us take it.

Make him pay for more line, he thought. Make him pay for it.

He could not see the fish's jumps but only heard the breaking of the ocean and the heavy splash as he fell. The speed of the line was cutting his hands badly but he had always known this would happen and he tried to keep the cutting across the calloused parts and not let the line slip into the palm or cut the fingers.

The line went out and out and out but it was slowing now and he was making the fish earn each inch of it. Now he got his head up from the wood and out of the slice of fish that his cheek had crushed. Then he was on his knees and then he rose slowly to his feet. He was ceding line but more slowly all the time. He worked back to where he could feel with his foot the coils of line that he could not see. There was plenty of line still and now the fish had to pull the friction of all that new line through the water.

Yes, he thought. And now he has jumped more than a dozen times and filled the sacs along his back with air and he cannot go down deep to die where I cannot bring him up. He will start circling soon and then I must work on him. I wonder what started him so suddenly? Could it have been hunger that made him desperate, or was he frightened by something in the night? Maybe he suddenly felt fear. But he was such a calm, strong fish and he seemed so fearless and so confident. It is strange.

'You better be fearless and confident yourself, old man,' he said. 'You're holding him again but you cannot get line. But soon he has to circle.'

The old man held him with his left hand and his shoulders now and stooped down and scooped up water in his right hand to get the crushed dolphin flesh off of his face. He was afraid that it might nauseate him and he would vomit and lose his strength. When his face was cleaned he washed his right hand in the water over

the side and then let it stay in the salt water while he
watched the first light come before the sunrise. He's
headed almost east, he thought. That means he is tired
and going with the current. Soon he will have to circle.
Then our true work begins.

After he judged that his right hand had been in the
water long enough he took it out and looked at it.

'It is not bad,' he said. 'And pain does not matter to
a man.'

He took hold of the line carefully so that it did not
fit into any of the fresh line cuts and shifted his weight
so that he could put his left hand into the sea on the
other side of the skiff.

'You did not do so badly for something worthless,'
he said to his left hand. 'But there was a moment when
I could not find you.'

Why was I not born with two good hands? he
thought. Perhaps it was my fault in not training that
one properly. But God knows he has had enough
chances to learn. He did not do so badly in the night,
though, and he was only cramped once. If he cramps
again let the line cut him off.

When he thought that he knew that he was not
being clear-headed and he thought he should chew
some more of the dolphin. But I can't, he told himself.
It is better to be light-headed than to lose your strength
from nausea. And I know I cannot keep it if I eat it
since my face was in it. I will keep it for an emergency
until it goes bad. But it is too late to try for strength
now through nourishment. You're stupid, he told
himself. Eat the other flying fish.

It was there, cleaned and ready, and he picked it up
with his left hand and ate it chewing the bones carefully
and eating all of it down to the tail.

It has more nourishment than almost any fish, he

thought. At least the kind of strength that I need. Now I have done what I can, he thought. Let him begin to circle and let the fight come.

The sun was rising for the third time since he had put to sea when the fish started to circle.

He could not see by the slant of the line that the fish was circling. It was too early for that. He just felt a faint slackening of the pressure of the line and he commenced to pull on it gently with his right hand. It tightened, as always, but just when he reached the point where it would break, line began to come in. He slipped his shoulders and head from under the line and began to pull in line steadily and gently. He used both of his hands in a swinging motion and tried to do the pulling as much as he could with his body and his legs. His old legs and shoulders pivoted with the swinging of the pulling.

'It is a very big circle,' he said. 'But he is circling.'

Then the line would not come in any more and he held it until he saw the drops jumping from it in the sun. Then it started out and the old man knelt down and let it go grudgingly back into the dark water.

'He is making the far part of his circle now,' he said. I must hold all I can, he thought. The strain will shorten his circle each time. Perhaps in an hour I will see him. Now I must convince him and then I must kill him.

But the fish kept on circling slowly and the old man was wet with sweat and tired deep into his bones two hours later. But the circles were much shorter now and from the way the line slanted he could tell the fish had risen steadily while he swam.

For an hour the old man had been seeing black spots before his eyes and the sweat salted his eyes and salted the cut over his eye and on his forehead. He was not

afraid of the black spots. They were normal at the tension that he was pulling on the line. Twice, though, he had felt faint and dizzy and that had worried him.

'I could not fail myself and die on a fish like this,' he said. 'Now that I have him coming so beautifully, God help me endure. I'll say a hundred Our Fathers and a hundred Hail Marys. But I cannot say them now.'

Consider them said, he thought. I'll say them later.

Just then he felt a sudden banging and jerking on the line he held with his two hands. It was sharp and hard-feeling and heavy.

He is hitting the wire leader with his spear, he thought. That was bound to come. He had to do that. It may make him jump though and I would rather he stayed circling now. The jumps were necessary for him to take air. But after that each one can widen the opening of the hook wound and he can throw the hook.

'Don't jump, fish,' he said. 'Don't jump.'

The fish hit the wire several times more and each time he shook his head the old man gave up a little line.

I must hold his pain where it is, he thought. Mine does not matter. I can control mine. But his pain could drive him mad.

After a while the fish stopped beating at the wire and started circling slowly again. The old man was gaining line steadily now. But he felt faint again. He lifted some sea water with his left hand and put it on his head. Then he put more on and rubbed the back of his neck.

'I have no cramps,' he said. 'He'll be up soon and I can last. You have to last. Don't even speak of it.'

He kneeled against the bow and, for a moment, slipped the line over his back again. I'll rest now while

he goes out on the circle and then stand up and work on him when he comes in, he decided.

It was a great temptation to rest in the bow and let the fish make one circle by himself without recovering any line. But when the strain showed the fish had turned to come toward the boat, the old man rose to his feet and started the pivoting and the weaving pulling that brought in all the line he gained.

I'm tireder than I have ever been, he thought, and now the trade wind is rising. But that will be good to take him in with. I need that badly.

'I'll rest on the next turn as he goes out,' he said. 'I feel much better. Then in two or three turns more I will have him.'

His straw hat was far on the back of his head and he sank down into the bow with the pull of the line as he felt the fish turn.

You work now, fish, he thought. I'll take you at the turn.

The sea had risen considerably. But it was a fair-weather breeze and he had to have it to get home.

'I'll just steer south and west,' he said. 'A man is never lost at sea and it is a long island.'

It was on the third turn that he saw the fish first.

He saw him first as a dark shadow that took so long to pass under the boat that he could not believe its length.

'No,' he said. 'He can't be that big.'

But he was that big and at the end of this circle he came to the surface only thirty yards away and the man saw his tail out of water. It was higher than a big scythe blade and a very pale lavender above the dark blue water. It raked back and as the fish swam just below the surface the old man could see his huge bulk and the purple stripes that banded him. His dorsal fin was down and his huge pectorals were spread wide.

On this circle the old man could see the fish's eye and the two grey sucking fish that swam around him. Sometimes they attached themselves to him. Sometimes they darted off. Sometimes they would swim easily in his shadow. They were each over three feet long and when they swam fast they lashed their whole bodies like eels.

The old man was sweating now but from something else besides the sun. On each calm placid turn the fish made he was gaining line and he was sure that in two turns more he would have a chance to get the harpoon in.

But I must get him close, close, close, he thought. I mustn't try for the head. I must get the heart.

'Be calm and strong, old man,' he said.

On the next circle the fish's back was out but he was a little too far from the boat. On the next circle he was still too far away but he was higher out of water and the old man was sure that by gaining some more line he could have him alongside.

He had rigged his harpoon long before and its coil of light rope was in a round basket and the end was made fast to the bitt in the bow.

The fish was coming in on his circle now calm and beautiful-looking and only his great tail moving. The old man pulled on him all that he could to bring him closer. For just a moment the fish turned a little on his side. Then he straightened himself and began another circle.

'I moved him,' the old man said. 'I moved him then.'

He felt faint again now but he held on the great fish all the strain that he could. I moved him, he thought. Maybe this time I can get him over. Pull, hands, he thought. Hold up, legs. Last for me, head. Last for me. You never went. This time I'll pull him over.

But when he put all of his effort on, starting it well out before the fish came alongside and pulling with all his strength, the fish pulled part way over and then righted himself and swam away.

'Fish,' the old man said. 'Fish, you are going to have to die anyway. Do you have to kill me too?'

That way nothing is accomplished, he thought. His mouth was too dry to speak but he could not reach for the water now. I must get him alongside this time, he thought. I am not good for many more turns. Yes you are, he told himself. You're good for ever.

On the next turn he nearly had him. But again the fish righted himself and swam slowly away.

You are killing me, fish, the old man thought. But you have a right to. Never have I seen a greater, or more beautiful, or a calmer or more noble thing than you, brother. Come on and kill me. I do not care who kills who.

Now you are getting confused in the head, he thought. You must keep your head clear. Keep your head clear and know how to suffer like a man. Or a fish, he thought.

'Clear up, head,' he said in a voice he could hardly hear. 'Clear up.'

Twice more it was the same on the turns.

I do not know, the old man thought. He had been on the point of feeling himself go each time. I do not know. But I will try it once more.

He tried it once more and he felt himself going when he turned the fish. The fish righted himself and swam off again slowly with the great tail weaving in the air.

I'll try it again, the old man promised, although his hands were mushy now and he could only see well in flashes.

He tried it again and it was the same. So, he

thought, and he felt himself going before he started; I will try it once again.

He took all his pain and what was left of his strength and his long gone pride and he put it against the fish's agony and the fish came over on to his side and swam gently on his side, his bill almost touching the planking of the skiff, and started to pass the boat, long, deep, wide, silver and barred with purple and interminable in the water.

The old man dropped the line and put his foot on it and lifted the harpoon as high as he could and drove it down with all his strength, and more strength he had just summoned, into the fish's side just behind the great chest fin that rose high in the air to the altitude of the man's chest. He felt the iron go in and he leaned on it and drove it further and then pushed all his weight after it.

Then the fish came alive, with his death in him, and rose high out of the water showing all his great length and width and all his power and his beauty. He seemed to hang in the air above the old man in the skiff. Then he fell into the water with a crash that sent spray over the old man and over all of the skiff.

The old man felt faint and sick and he could not see well. But he cleared the harpoon line and let it run slowly through his raw hands and, when he could see, he saw the fish was on his back with his silver belly up. The shaft of the harpoon was projecting at an angle from the fish's shoulder and the sea was discolouring with the red of the blood from his heart. First it was dark as a shoal in the blue water that was more than a mile deep. Then it spread like a cloud. The fish was silvery and still and floated with the waves.

The old man looked carefully in the glimpse of vision that he had. Then he took two turns of the

harpoon line around the bitt in the bow and laid his head on his hand.

'Keep my head clear,' he said against the wood of the bow. 'I am a tired old man. But I have killed this fish which is my brother and now I must do the slave work.'

Now I must prepare the nooses and the rope to lash him alongside, he thought. Even if we were two and swamped her to load him and bailed her out, this skiff would never hold him. I must prepare everything, then bring him in and lash him well and step the mast and set sail for home.

He started to pull the fish in to have him alongside so that he could pass a line through his gills and out of his mouth and make his head fast alongside the bow. I want to see him, he thought, and to touch and to feel him. He is my fortune, he thought. But that is not why I wish to feel him. I think I felt his heart, he thought. When I pushed on the harpoon shaft the second time. Bring him in now and make him fast and get the noose around his tail and another around his middle to bind him to the skiff.

'Get to work, old man,' he said. He took a very small drink of the water. 'There is very much slave work to be done now that the fight is over.'

He looked up at the sky and then out to his fish. He looked at the sun carefully. It is not much more than noon, he thought. And the trade wind is rising. The lines all mean nothing now.

'Come on, fish,' he said. But the fish did not come. Instead he lay there wallowing now in the seas and the old man pulled the skiff up on to him.

When he was even with him and had the fish's head against the bow he could not believe his size. But he untied the harpoon rope from the bitt, passed it

through the fish's gills and out of his jaws, made a turn around his sword then passed the rope through the other gill, made another turn around the bill and knotted the double rope and made it fast to the bitt in the bow. He cut the rope then and went astern to noose the tail. The fish had turned silver from his original purple and silver, and the stripes showed the same pale violet colour as his tail. They were wider than a man's hand with his fingers spread and the fish's eye looked as detached as the mirrors in a periscope or as a saint in a procession.

'It was the only way to kill him,' the old man said. He was feeling better since the water and he knew he would not go away and his head was clear. He's over fifteen hundred pounds the way he is, he thought. Maybe much more. If he dresses out two-thirds of that at thirty cents a pound?

'I need a pencil for that,' he said. 'My head is not that clear. But I think the great DiMaggio would be proud of me today. I had no bone spurs. But the hands and the back hurt truly.' I wonder what a bone spur is, he thought. Maybe we have them without knowing of it.

He made the fish fast to bow and stern and to the middle thwart. He was so big it was like lashing a much bigger skiff alongside. He cut a piece of line and tied the fish's lower jaw against his bill so his mouth would not open and they would sail as cleanly as possible. Then he stepped the mast and, with the stick that was his gaff and with his boom rigged, the patched sail drew, the boat began to move, and half lying in the stern he sailed south-west.

Woman Skating

A lake sunken among
cedar and black spruce hills;
late afternoon.

On the ice a woman skating,
jacket sudden
red against the white,

concentrating on moving
in perfect circles.

    (actually she is my mother, she is over at the
    outdoor skating rink near the cemetery. On
    three sides of her there are streets of brown
    brick houses; cars go by; on the fourth side is
    the park building. The snow banked around
    the rink is grey with soot. She never skates
    here. She's wearing a sweater and faded
    maroon earmuffs, she has taken off her
    gloves)

Now near the horizon
the enlarged pink sun swings down.
Soon it will be zero.

With arms wide the skater
turns, leaving her breath like a diver's
trail of bubbles.

Seeing the ice
as what it is, water:
seeing the months
as they are, the years
in sequence occurring
underfoot, watching
the miniature human
figure balanced on steel
needles (those compasses
floated in saucers) on time
sustained, above
time circling: miracle

Over all I place
a glass bell

Margaret Atwood

The Ice Hockey Stick

GLYNN ARTHUR LEYSHON

Sitting on the kerb in the fading light, Mannie leaned his weight forward and aimed a glob of spit at the dust between his feet in the gutter. He reflected on the game just ended. Ball hockey on the road wasn't the same as the real thing. Even here, though, he had taken his lumps. Smaller than the rest, and squint-eyed to boot, he had to rely on cunning to play, because he wasn't even fast to make up for his lack of size. He sometimes had trouble, too, seeing the ball with his peripheral vision. He spat again. 'Dirty', they called him. 'Dirty.' He'd show them someday. When he was in the NHL and they were watching on TV.

'Mannie. Mandrake. Time for supper,' called his mother.

'Coming,' he yelled. 'Coming.'

As Mannie picked up his stick, he noticed a black cat across the street crouched in the gloom. Idly, he toed out a pebble and with his curved blade, flicked it towards the animal. The cat flinched but didn't move. He took another pebble and tried again with the same

result. Still feeling the frustrations of the game, he raised his stick and charged the cat uttering a growl. The cat hesitated, hissed at him, and finally fled.

Mannie skidded to a stop as something clattered underfoot. He saw it was a ratty-looking stick. Someone must have forgotten it after the game. In the bad light it was hard to see the initials on it. It wasn't very good, but it was whole, no cracks in the blade. He decided to take it. Might come in handy. A broken stick puts you out of the games. As he hefted it, it seemed to thrum. It felt the way a stick feels when it has been hammered on the pavement. A sort of vibration went through it. Mannie wasn't sure he had even felt it. He propped the black stick over his shoulder with his own, and puffed a steamy breath towards home. As he ran his hand idly down the shaft, he noticed that instead of the usual knob of tape on the end there was a band of metal, iron or something.

Mannie stacked the stick with his hockey equipment barely noting that it was black and that the heel seemed different somehow. As he removed his jacket, the sleeve brushed the black stick and it slid to the floor with a small bang. He didn't bother to pick it up. Supper was wafting from the kitchen.

The Red Circle League was formed on the premiss that every kid should have equal ice time. A buzzer, in fact, sounded every three minutes so that coaches could have no excuse for not changing lines. In practice, nearly every coach bent the rules and some, like Mannie's, fractured them altogether. He switched sweaters, pretended injuries, and simply lied about which player had been on the ice. He burned to win and treated team Mother Tuckers as candidates for the Stanley Cup; therefore, he played what he thought were his

best players as much as possible and the rest sat with
their chins on the boards, noses streaming in the cold,
waiting impatiently for the call when Coach Taylor
could deny them no longer. When he had to put them
in, Little Mannie with the bad eyes was one of the last
to get a shift.

It did not take much for Mannie to realize that he
wasn't coach Taylor's favourite. Once he heard him
say, 'That kid Mannie. He's got dancing eyes. Except
one's on the bridge of his nose sitting this one out. Ha,
ha, ha.' Mannie had pretended not to hear, and on his
next shift butt-ended his opposite number and was
banished from the game. The coach told everyone that
Mannie was the team's enforcer. His mother was quite
upset. She came loyally to every game and suffered
silently with her son at his lack of ice time, but she
scolded him for his penalties and fighting.

'OK. Furtney's line. Get out there,' came the call.

'Yeah,' Mannie grunted. He edged his way to the
gate. His line mates climbed over the boards and were
gone. Mannie bucked the stream of players coming in.
He was bumped, lost his balance, and sat heavily on
the bench again. Thrusting up, furious, he began to
flail with his elbows. He had to reach the ice.

'C'mon, Mannie, for Chrissake!' came the cry.

'Lemme out, you goddamn guys.'

Finally, Mannie popped through the opening,
wobbled as he hit the ice, and then laboured to his
wing as the play developed.

'Eggs' Furtney, the centre, was a pretty good skater.
The only reason he was teamed with Mannie was that
Furtney did not like the contact. He never went into
the corners and he never won a face off. He was like a
beautiful, darting butterfly swooping in and out, never
stopping, and always willing to give up the puck in

exchange for contact immunity. As the saying went, 'He could go into the corner with a pocketful of eggs and come out without staining his pants'. Mannie went into the corners, was knocked flat, rose, and launched himself into the mêlée again and again.

A long pass fluttered past 'Eggs' and into the boards. Mannie skated desperately to dig it out. The defence man hammered him in the shoulder and he just caught his balance in time. The puck was trapped. Mannie pushed with all his strength against his man, and felt another body come in behind him. Thump. He caught an elbow in the back and his head whiplashed into the man in front. For an instant, his face mask caught on the fabric of the baggy hockey pants. Mannie could see the weave of the material, the contrasting stripe of red. Then he was forced to the ice. He dropped his stick.

God, how he hated to drop his stick. The big gloves and his small hands conspired against him. He couldn't pinch the wood hard enough to pick it up. The stick slid teasingly. He tried again, but it squirted away like a piece of wet soap. He had to ignore the game for a moment, and on all fours, sobbing with humiliation, push the stick to the boards where it would stop sliding, and then push it up until he could get his fingers under and around it at last. He was enraged with frustration at this point.

From all fours, he could see the puck clearly through the tangle of sticks and legs. He tried to stand, but someone stumbled over him. He crawled towards the puck, pulling himself along by grabbing the occasional leg. Someone settled slowly on top of him with a suffocating weight. Mannie flailed with his elbows, rose to his knees, and in fury aimed a two-hander at the nearest body. He missed. His stick struck the boards and shattered. Mannie's heart sank.

Head down, he skated to the bench carrying the broken stick. Narrow shoulders slumped, he eased through the gate. No stick; no play. He knew that. No stick; no play. Easy to remember. He bit his lip to keep it from trembling. He was ready to punch the first person to speak.

'Mandrake.' He whirled, fists up. It was his mother behind the bench. He wished she wouldn't call him that.

'Mandrake. Do you need this?' and she held up the black monstrosity he had found on the street. The heavy, awkward, black stick with a metal band on it. He hadn't even thought about taping it. It was a pretty ugly piece of equipment.

'I thought you forgot it,' said his mother. 'It was standing up where you left it.'

Mannie hesitated. He already took enough from them. His scrawny body, his crossed eyes, his lack of speed. One more thing. The stick was one more thing. But without it, he couldn't get on the ice at all. He had to get into the play. He had to show them. Thrusting out his jaw, he snatched the stick and turned away.

'Say one goddamn word, "Eggs", and you'll be spittin' teeth.'

Resentment surrounded him like an aura; it radiated from him as he glanced around. Fortunately, everyone was engrossed in the game. He sat down with the stick between his knees, his teeth set in a grimace. Every stringy muscle in his banty-rooster body was rigid and taut. 'And that goes for the rest of you bastards, too,' he mumbled to himself.

Between periods Coach Taylor blasted them. This was one of the few times that Mannie was like the rest. Everyone took it from Coach Taylor. He was into it now.

'Mother Tuckers. I'll tell you what. You're a bunch,

all right, but you ain't a bunch of Mother Tuckers. You're a bunch of goddam guys! I never seen such a lousy game in my life. If you bastards think for one minute that you've been in a hockey game then you must a been hit in the head. Come to think of it, if you was hit in the head it must have been on the way here 'cause sure as shit no one got hit in this game. The whole damn bunch of you should be called "Eggs".'

Mannie writhed and fidgeted. He hated this kind of talk. He hated worse to lose. And they were losing. If they'd just let him play a bit more he'd knock a few people down. Just let me play, he thought.

As the third period began, Mannie's heart sank although he wouldn't let anyone see his despair. Coach Taylor took one look at the black stick. 'Jeesus Kaarist. What the hell is that you're draggin' around? Ain't got a proper heel. Got a weird lie. And where's your tape knob? You 'spect to play with that thing, Mannie, or fix a picket fence someplace. Ha, ha, ha.'

When the centre on the first line slid into the boards and hurt his leg, Coach Taylor had to start juggling his lines. Even 'Eggs' was given more ice time. With a penalty to a winger, Coach Taylor looked down the bench to the hard-eyed Mannie and reluctantly gave him the sign. He stumbled in his eagerness, his skates catching in the rubber strip of the laneway to the gate. But he was on the ice.

'Geez, I wish that kid would climb over the boards like everyone else,' said Coach Taylor to no one in particular. 'A player that can't climb out looks like a pile of puppy-shit.'

As soon as his stick touched the ice, Mannie felt something. Subtle but there, he sensed a kind of vibration and suddenly the stick no longer seemed heavy. It was hard to tell exactly, but Mannie felt as he

did when his skates were freshly sharpened and the ice was resurfaced. He moved further then with each thrust. He could glide longer. There seemed almost no friction. He had that sensation now.

Quickly he caught up with the play. Quicker, it seemed to him than ever before. He drove into the tangle of players in the corner. The puck, trapped amid skates and sticks, seemed to defy all efforts to gain it. Motionless, it was tantalizingly out of reach even though it was close. Hands, knees, sticks, skates were all counter-balanced one by another. No one could extricate enough of himself to extend the last few inches to possession.

Grunting and cursing the group swayed and fought. Mannie hit them like a bowling ball. Through the scattering bodies, he reached his stick to the puck. Did his eyes deceive him? For a brief second it looked to him that the stick extended. Absurd. A stick cannot grow. Yet, he hooked the puck clear before anyone else got to it. Not only that, it seemed almost attracted to his blade. Like a magnet.

With swelling confidence, Mannie wheeled out of the corner and headed for the slot. No one to centre it to so he kept the puck. A defenceman chopped at his stick, but it did not have an effect. Another came under and lifted the black crescent of his blade, but the puck glided on and he retrieved it without effort. He shot. A wrist shot that sped towards the goalie then hooked to the short side and went in over his stick arm. Goal! The light went on. Goal! He had scored! Oh God, what a feeling. Drunk with excitement he spun in a circle, his stick raised like a black triumphant obelisk. A goal. He had never felt so light, so high, so good. A goal. Did it always feel this way? What had he been missing?

'Yah, Mannie. Way ta go, Mannie,' came the

booming sound of Coach Taylor's voice. 'Mother Tucker's all the way!'

His team mates crowded him, slapping his hand, clapping him on the helmet, hugging him. The black stick, its odd blade back on the ice, hummed in his gloved hand, but he barely noticed. With a dazed half smile he headed for the bench as the shouts diminished. He did not need a rest. There was no effort to his motion. Gracefully, he pumped to the entrance, his black stick light and whippy in his hand. Maybe they'd let him on again, soon. The intoxication of the moment made him long like an addict for another hit.

With a new look in his eyes Coach Taylor yelled for Mannie again. He left 'Eggs' on the bench and teamed Mannie with a centre from another line. This time out Mannie took a pass as he crossed centre, and sped up his wing. He couldn't swear to it, but his stick out in front seemed to pull him along. He was on the verge of losing control, pulled along faster than his skates could keep up. The black stick seemed to hum in his hands, to sing tunelessly to him. The tempo increased. He blew past the defenceman who lunged at him and tried to poke check the puck away. Faster and faster he went. The goal loomed up and the goalie came out to challenge. Mannie rocketed towards him, the blade of his stick moving the puck from side to side almost on its own. He deked with his shoulders then flicked a wrist shot to the five hole. Zap. The net bulged. The light went on. Mannie swooped away one knee raised, his free arm pumping. It was over so fast he was unsure of anything except that he had scored and the elation filled him to overflowing. What a feeling! He could never get enough.

On his next shift, he completed the hat trick with a deflection on a shot from the point. Before the game

ended, he scored twice more. Even Coach Taylor treated him differently. Five goals put him up there with the best. Five goals bought ice time to score more goals. Mannie had never experienced this excitement. His eyes glowed and his heart pumped. He would take hours to fall asleep.

In the next two games, Mannie scored eight times. Coach Taylor sat him near the gate now so that he could get on the ice sooner. He was a long way from the end where the back-up goalie and 'Eggs' Furtney sat. Scoring goals changed everything. By the time the season was half over Mannie had a better than four goals a game average and had been picked to play on an all-star team against a similar group from Quebec. There had even been a newspaper article comparing him to Gretzky at the same age. It noted Mannie's scoring average was about the same as the 'Great One's'.

Without telling anyone or admitting it to himself, Mannie sensed that the black stick had changed something for him. Maybe it was his luck. He tried putting a tape knob on the stick, but somehow, the tape disappeared. It did not seem to adhere over the narrow band of metal on the butt-end. The same happened to the blade. Everyone taped his own blade especially after warping it over a stove element. The curves could be custom made that way then strengthened with electrician's tape. But not the black stick. The tape slid off before a single shift was over. Mannie had watched it split and slough like the skin of a garter snake. Nothing seemed to stick to the surface of the black stick.

He practised with it constantly. When there were no morning practices, he rose at 6:30 and began shooting at the net he had drawn on the garage wall. Thud,

thud, thud. The block of rubber bruised the concrete. He never missed. He could hit any corner or the five hole with uncanny accuracy. A current seemed to flow from the black blade. He looked at the top right corner and flicked his wrists. The puck rose instantly and thudded an inch under the crossbar. He tried slap shots, but had to limit them. The noise and the vibration inside the house kept his mother on edge. Once he had made a cake fall. The slap shot would surely tear through the netting of a real goal. It chipped the concrete of the garage wall.

Despite his growing fame, Mannie still played road hockey—and always the black stick accompanied him. Things were different even in the street games. He was always first pick if, indeed, he wasn't one of the captains. Scrawny, his head turned slightly to one side to see better, he looked disdainfully at his former tormentors. He let them squirm as he flicked his eyes down the ragged line.

'You,' he would bark and give a toss of his head. The one he indicated would be delighted to scamper to his side. Everyone likes to go with a winner.

In the street games all had felt the wrath of the black stick. If Mannie could score five or six goals in a regular game he could easily double that in a pick-up game of road hockey. Nothing could stand in his way. When he did not have the ball, he often hacked his way to it. Like the puck, the ball seemed to cling to the blade of the black stick. A ball is harder to stick handle than a puck, but Mannie, if anything, seemed better with the ball. He could fake a shot, drop his shoulder, pivot, toe the ball between his feet and be gone shuffling up the asphalt to the goal. Once in the clear the result was foregone. He never missed. And even in the street games he exulted.

Mother Tuckers was in first place thanks largely to Mannie's scoring. The playoffs were approaching and Coach Taylor was expansive as winners can be. He paced around the locker room.

'Mannie, my boy. Mannie. I'm gonna try you between Jack and Syl tonight. Maybe you pot ten, tonight. Ha, ha, ha.'

'Yeah,' Mannie grunted bent over his skates. He felt a wave of irritation. What did this fat bastard know about it, anyway?

'Ya hear me, Mannie. That OK with you?'

'Yeah,' said Mannie without looking up. It didn't matter much who they put on his line. He'd score anyway. He'd score and score and, snap, he broke his lace. 'Goddamn,' he shouted. Startled faces looked over.

'What is it, Mannie. What's the matter?' said Coach Taylor.

'Nuthing. Nuthin',' replied Mannie, hard-eyed. 'Nuthin'. Gimme another lace.'

In the first few minutes of the game, Mannie intercepted a pass in the high slot area in front of his net and headed up ice. No winger could match his new-found speed and he jetted along behind his stick, alone. In a blink he was in front of the cowering goalie. Instead of shooting, he circled the net, the goalie's head pivoting like an owl's to follow him and came out in front skating away towards his own goal. Stopping suddenly in a shower of ice, he shot blind and backhanded while looking at his own advancing players. The confused goalie, his mouth agape, didn't even see the puck burst past his idle catching hand. Mannie had scored on a breakaway while looking at his own goalie. The black stick purred in his hand and a tingling sensation passed through his gloves.

He did a little dance on his skates as his team clustered to him like filings to a magnet. Most were bigger and they reached down to tap his helmet or punch his shoulder. Everyone was lifted by the performance except the other team. The goalie hung his head and carefully cleaned the goal area of imagined debris. Mannie scored nine more that night, and the newspaper did a feature on him complete with comments from an NHL scout.

Later, after he had carefully dried his skate blades and hung his equipment to dry, Mannie sat in the kitchen with his mother drinking hot chocolate.

'Mandrake, why is your stick in the kitchen?' asked his mother.

'I—uh—I guess I just—' mumbled Mannie. He could not remember bringing the stick with him, but he must have. It stood against the wall, battered and black, with a kind of glow to it. He rose, grasped the stick and carried it out to the garage. Jamming it against the wall he felt a momentary irritation. He was tired. He would sleep in tomorrow. Missing one day wouldn't make any difference. He walked slowly back to finish his hot drink before going to bed.

At 6:30 next morning, a crash awakened Mannie. Startled, he sat upright in bed, his heart thumping.

'Mandrake. What was that?' called his mother.

'Dunno.'

'It sounded like it came from the garage,' said his mother.

'I'll take a look.'

Mannie climbed from bed and walked to the garage. He peered in and saw nothing untoward. True, his black stick had fallen over, but that shouldn't have made all that noise. He hesitated then walked over to stand the stick upright. As he touched it, his fingers

were pulled around it in a death grip. His heart beat
faster. Without being aware, he slipped on his boots,
flipped a puck over the sill, and was outside eyeing his
target. He began shooting. Thump, top right; thump,
top left; thump, lower right. With a trance-like
blankness, he shot. He shot from sharp angles,
forehand, backhand and always effortlessly and with
power. The puck was unerring.

'Mandrake. What are you doing out here in
pyjamas,' said his mother. 'Come into the house right
away. This is ridiculous.'

Mannie was startled. He looked at his mother as
though coming from a deep sleep. He stared down at
his pyjamas and quickly around at the bare and empty
street.

'I—uh—I guess I forgot,' he whispered. Shivering,
he followed his mother inside, carefully standing the
stick in its customary place.

Tonight the playoffs would start. The first game of a
best-of-five semi-final. He looked at the stick for a minute
before going to breakfast. Black. It was very black.

In the opening period, Mannie was manhandled.
Twice he was grabbed and hauled down to the ice,
players piling on top.

'The bastards. They're trying to put him outta the
game,' shouted Coach Taylor. 'Well, we'll see about
that.'

When Mannie finished his shift and sat down, Coach
Taylor leaned over him.

'Keep taking that shit and you're gonna get hurt,
Mannie. This ain't like you. Don't take it. Make some
space. Do a little stick work on them bastards. Lay the
lumber to 'em,' he growled.

On his next shift, Mannie took the puck on a clearing pass and hit centre ice in full stride. He faked right and got the defenceman leaning and then with incredible swiftness cut to his left. As he crossed the blue line he triggered a slapshot. The stick was alive in his hands. The vibration was the highest he had known—it was almost audible. The shot had all his momentum behind it and it rose bullet-like from his blade. Incredibly, it not only erupted into the netting behind the hapless goalkeeper, it ripped through the fabric, hit the end glass and smashed the panel in front of the goal judge. Everyone said there must have been a skate cut in the netting, and maybe there was. No one could explain the shattering of the supposedly unbreakable panel except to say that it, too, must have had a flaw in it. It took several minutes to restore order. The goal judge was shaken by the experience and had to be replaced.

As the game progressed, Mannie was harassed more and more in action away from the puck. 'Give it back to 'em, Mannie,' said Coach Taylor. 'This ain't like you. Make 'em back off.'

After taking a heavy elbow to the head and a mauling from behind Mannie retaliated in exasperation. He had never had to use the black stick this way before. Had had no occasion. But now, in a flood of resentment he thrust at one of his tormentors. The black blade flashed like a scimitar and the boy collapsed screaming and holding his gut. The referee was screened, so no penalty was called. The injured player was taken by ambulance to have his ruptured spleen removed. The harassment ceased, and Mannie scored a hat trick in that period alone.

'Way ta go, Mannie. We'll teach those sons-a-bitches,' shouted Coach Taylor. 'Nobuddy messes with Mother Tuckers.'

Mother Tuckers swept the best of five in three straight and rested while the other series continued. They would play the winner of it for the title in a best-of-seven set-up.

Although he had scored an astonishing six goals per game in the semi-final series, Mannie continued to arise each morning and feverishly pepper the garage wall. He played road hockey, too, with a ruthless ferocity. Twice when he approached to join a game already started, it dissolved, the players walking sullenly away shouldering the nets or dragging their sticks.

At home, Mannie became more withdrawn. His mother noted that he often sat staring blankly. She worried that his already thin body appeared to be getting thinner, but she knew that he was strung tight, too tight to talk to. Maybe after they won the championship. Only a few more days.

The first game of the final series was barely under way when the coach of the opposing team, Thompson Trucking, requested that Mannie's stick be measured. He was sure the curve in the blade exceeded the regulations. How else could one account for a shot that scored from the corner back of the net. It had curved in under the crossbar.

Mannie watched as, for the first time, someone else held his stick. He skated behind the official to the scorer's table where the measuring instrument lay.

'God, this thing is heavy,' said the referee. 'I don't know how you play with it, son.'

The referee measured the stick.

'You're right, coach. It is illegal. That's a penalty to Mother Tuckers.'

'Wait a minute,' Mannie heard himself say. 'Wait a minute. Show me.'

As the official put the ruler on the stick Mannie saw

the blade uncurl like a slowly turned page. By the time
it was measured the blade was straight as a plumb line.

'We'll I'll be damned,' said the referee. 'I can't
believe this. I just measured and—I must be seeing
things. It . . . it—naw. It couldn't straighten itself out.
I musta made a mistake. Sorry, son.'

As the game continued, Mannie sense an increased
electricity in the stick. His hands tingled constantly, and
he could feel it through his scrawny body. It possessed
him. He was everywhere on the ice. Blades flashing, he
swooped from one end to the other. He killed penalties,
worked on the power play and took his regular shift
besides. He even worked a 'loft' play in which a
defenceman would lob the puck over the opposition and
into their zone. Given a few milliseconds of hang time,
the puck would descend to the ice just as Mannie burst
over the blue line to pick it up. It was devastating to
Thompson Trucking. Big and physical in their
approach, they were bewildered by the play. There was
no one to hit in the corners.

When Mannie got the puck on a loft play, he was
often wide open in front of the goalie. The first blast he
took from this position scored, but only after striking
the goalie in the throat and lifting him off his feet.
The puck trickled inexorably across the line as the
gasping goal tender lost consciousness. His replacement
strapped on his gear with great reluctance.

Mannie sat on the bench breathing heavily and
sweating, his drawn face set after scoring his fourth
goal. There was little delight now. Everyone expected
him to score. He was Mother Tuckers. He was the
hockey team. The high fives were perfunctory; the
helmet taps routine. They were already anticipating the
end. Mother Tuckers won the game 9–3 and Mannie
had eight goals.

At the second game, an NHL scout was in the stands. Mannie's scoring had made the wire service. He interested the pros despite his tender age and the league he was in. His mother, of course, was in the stands, as well. She was interested in his health. She saw not a unique scoring machine, but a pale, thin boy with feverish eyes and a grim set to his face.

Mother Tuckers won the second and third games as easily as the first. Mannie outscored the other team by a wide margin. The newspaper even reported the wins as 'Mannie Tuckers' against Thompson Trucking. The fourth game was a foregone conclusion. Who could stop this juggernaut? A four game sweep of the series was inevitable.

Mannie, if it were possible, was strung tighter than before. The stick never seemed to leave his grasp. Between games, he played road hockey whenever the game didn't dissolve at his approach, and mornings and sometimes after school, the steady thud of the puck against the garage wall told his mother his whereabouts. The stick now spent the nights against the wall in Mannie's bedroom where with staring eyes, he could see it glowing faintly in the dark. What more did it want?

The final game in the championship series took place on a warm Saturday in April. Mannie played with frenzied energy in spite of the heat. He was everywhere and did everything at a more frantic pace than ever. Twice on penalties in the first period, Thompson Trucking did not get a single shot on goal. When Mannie killed penalties it was as though they weren't a man short. The despondent Thompson team started to rough things up in their frustration and that led to many penalties. Mannie, of course, played on the power play and the scoring opportunities increased for him.

He scored from the slot; he scored from the point; once, from behind the net, he flicked the puck up against the goalie's head and watched it roll down his back to score. The game was an anticlimax as Mother Tuckers won 11–0.

Mannie's mother sighed as the game ended. Now at last Mannie could relax. Now he could take some of the pressure off himself. He could get away from hockey for a while. Maybe they could go for a visit with her sister. As she waited for him in the corridor to drive him home she thought of all the things she might do with her son. The summer was coming. It would be a change. Get away from hockey. He could bask in his new-found glory for a while. He could relax. He could eat more and put on weight. Yes, she was glad it was over. Glad that Mannie could take the pressure off himself. She felt relieved.

The next morning, she awoke to a familiar sound. She peered from the window to see her son desperately firing a puck at the chipped concrete wall, his face contorted. She thought he might even be weeping as he gripped the black stick and drew back for another shot.

The Lady Pitcher

It is the last of the ninth, two down,
bases loaded, seventh
Game of the Series and here she comes, walking
On water,
Promising miracles. What a relief
Pitcher she has been all year.
Will she win it all now or
will this be the big bust which
She secures in wire and net beneath her uniform,
Wire and net like a double
Vision version
Of the sandlot homeplate backstop in Indiana where
She became known as Flameball Millie.

Cynthia Macdonald

To a Woman Caving

Backbone to rockbone; the
pitch of commitment, the
total cave;

relief tempered with
fear.

The unmoving contours of
rockface, the
grip and
flex of limbs; and
everywhere the
water echo into limestone
caverns;

stalagmites and
stalactites, the flower-glass of
stems,
embedded in this
cove, this close dark,

your own exhilarated
blood and
taliswoman limbs,
primal, new

Linda Rose Parkes

The Gymnast

SHEILA HAIGH

She climbed like a monkey up the iron structure that supported the girder against the factory wall. Passing a window, she flattened herself against the wall. Supposing someone in the factory saw her? Unlikely, since it appeared dark inside. Perhaps the factory didn't work on Sundays.

The iron was rusty and stained her clothes. Lucky she was wearing old jeans and the dirty trainers that Moira hated.

With a rush of adrenalin she reached the girder. It was wider than a beam, at least eight inches wide. Anda's eyes shone as she stepped on it. She loved it. High in the air above the water. Fifteen feet above the water. If I were not a gymnast, I'd be a bird!

The girder was firm under her feet. But just as David had warned, she felt disorientated being so high up. She sat astride it and took off her shoes and socks. Then she tied the laces together and hung them over the girder.

David and Julienne were still chatting in the tree. Good. She didn't want them to notice her until she'd

had a practice. Steady does it, I don't really want to fall, she thought, and walked across first to see how it felt. She tried to imagine blue crash mats underneath her, not cold water.

With a deep breath, looking straight ahead, she turned and ran back, her balance one hundred per cent. She tried a few dance steps and turns. Difficult on the slightly rusty surface. She did a few rolls to straddle. Easy. Now she could be more ambitious. Recklessly, she moved to the centre of the girder where she was over the water. Not daring to look down, she tried a walkover. Perfect. So perfect she did walkovers slowly all the way across. Lovely to be out in the sunshine, without Ian Barst shouting at her.

Exhilarated, she contemplated a back flip.

'Anda's a long time,' said Julienne, swinging her legs round the willow tree.

David sat facing her.

'She knows her way around.'

'Maybe we should go and meet her. She's in a funny mood,' said Julienne, jumping down from the tree.

'I don't know what's the matter with her.' David stayed in the tree. 'She was all right until you came!'

'Thanks very much!'

'No, I didn't mean it like that!'

'She gets like this at home,' said Julienne. 'She has a blazing row with her mum and she goes off and does gymnastics on top of the hill!'

David frowned.

'Yes—she threatened to . . . ' He looked up and saw a tiny figure doing walkovers on the girder, fifteen feet above the canal!

'Oh my God!' he yelled. 'Anda!'

Julienne stared in horror. Anda had done lots of mad things, but this had to be the worst.

'Flaming stupid, stupid little idiot!' roared David, giving full vent to his lungs.

'She can't hear us! We must get her down!' cried Julienne. 'She must be stopped! Don't yell at her, David. You'll put her off balance!'

But David had gone running down the towpath like an angry bull.

'You idiot! Don't do it, Anda! Don't!'

'For God's sake!' Julienne hared after him.

Anda heard David's angry yell just as she took off for a back flip. She landed shakily, wobbled, and almost fell.

Julienne screamed.

'Shut up, David. You'll make her worse!'

Shaken, Anda sat for a minute, astride the girder. She saw Julienne and David running down the towpath.

I can do better flips than that! she thought angrily.

She stood up, stretched and tried again.

'Anda! *No!*'

Perfect.

'Don't do any more!' pleaded Julienne.

'You get down here or I'll never speak to you again!' roared David.

But Anda was not stopping now.

Skilfully she did a walkover, followed by a flip.

She'd intended to do two flips but something sharp on the girder caught her foot. It threw her right off balance.

Crack! Her skull slammed against the iron girder. The sun swung like a pendulum. The factory walls rushed past. Anda blacked out and fell like a rag doll into the canal.

. . .

'She'll need to rest for at least a week.'

'We'll have to send her home.'

That finished it, Anda thought, hearing the voices through fogs of pain, that was the end of her training with Ian Barst. I've really blown it. With a surge of fear, she remembered falling from the girder. Gingerly she moved her legs and arms. Nothing was broken. I'm in hospital, was the next panicky thought. She opened her eyes a discreet slit. Moira was standing by the bed, chatting to a smiling Irish nurse.

'I'm giving up gymnastics,' she mumbled. At least I'm alive, she thought gratefully. To give up would be easy. A vivid picture of home came to her. She wanted desperately to go home.

'She's coming to at last!'

The smiling nurse leaned over her. She had such a merry freckled face and kind eyes that Anda couldn't help feeling safe with her, despite her fears about hospital.

'How do you feel, Anda?'

'I've got an awful headache. And my chest is wheezy,' said Anda.

'You've got concussion. You'll be quite all right in a day or so. You lie quiet. I'll get the doctor to have a look at you.'

'Doctor!' Anda looked startled. 'What is he going to do?'

'Oh, don't worry! Only shine a little torch in your eyes and listen to your chest. That's all.'

The nurse disappeared and Moira came to sit on the bed. She looked shaken and upset.

'Hey, don't worry, Auntie Moira! I'm sorry.'

'I'm sorry too!' sobbed Moira, dabbing her face with a screwed-up tissue. 'I know I should be bright and cheerful now, but I've been frantic about you, Anda. I was afraid you were going to be brain-damaged or something!'

Anda grinned reassuringly.

'My brain's not that brilliant anyway, so why worry!'

Moira was silent for a moment.

'You're a nice kid.' She took Anda's hand. 'And I know you think I'm a fusspot but I *do* care, you see. I'm sorry if you've had a rotten time in London.'

Anda digested this in surprise. She had misjudged Moira.

'It's not been easy, bringing David up on my own,' said Moira.

'No. I suppose it hasn't.' Anda closed her eyes again. All this emotion was not exactly what she needed right now.

'Don't give up gymnastics,' pleaded Moira. 'You're so good. You'll get over this! And did you know David saved your life? He was a real hero!'

'And I was a silly fool,' sighed Anda, 'to dance on that girder. I'm sorry I've caused so much trouble. And please, please don't tell my parents!'

'We already have, Anda. We had to. They're on the way up here!'

'Are they mad?'

'No, of course not! And guess what?'

'What?'

'Gran has invited David down to stay for the last week of the holidays.'

'Good! What about Julienne? Is she mad with me?'

'No. She'll be in to see you later. She was pretty shocked herself.'

'I left my shoes hanging on the girder! Lynne'll go mad.'

Worries loomed and flashed by like lorries on the motorway. What would Gran say? And Christie? Would she dare go back to Ferndale after this?'

She did dare. Two days before the Club Competition.

A sunlit week at Hooty Cottage had restored her to full strength, and the dreadful incident when she had almost drowned had faded in her mind. London seemed like a dream. Ian Barst's voice had stopped barking in her head. She felt glad just to be home, to hear the bees and the stream, and to cuddle Bella's soft sun-warmed fur.

David was enjoying his week with Gran. Impressed by his heroic rescue, Gran had made a fuss of him, and both were benefiting.

'It's time I got to know my brave grandson better!' she said, beaming.

As soon as Anda walked into Ferndale Gym Club on the Thursday evening, she felt truly at home. The atmosphere of a happy, well-disciplined gym club struck her instantly. It felt so friendly and welcoming that when Christie came and gave her a hug, she almost cried.

'We didn't expect you back so soon!'

'Hi, Anda!'

'Glad you're back!'

'We've missed you!'

All those dear faces surrounded her. Kerry, Elizabeth, John, and Christie. And Julienne stood beside her, beaming. No one mentioned her embarrassing accident. And no one mentioned her not completing the course with Ian Barst. She felt profoundly grateful for their tact.

'This is David,' she said brightly, pushing him forward. 'He's a boy . . . '

Everyone laughed, and David bowed, enjoying the limelight.

'Yes, we can see that!' said Christie, smiling.

'A boy gymnast, I was going to say!' cried Anda.

'Oh! A boy gymnast! Marvellous! Come *in*!' John bounded forward. 'We don't have enough of those around here! Are you going to give us a display on Saturday?'

David hesitated.

'We've got a pommel horse.'

'And a high bar!'

'I think we've got some rings put away somewhere too.'

'Oh go on, David!'

'OK.' He looked pleased. 'But don't expect much!'

'He's brilliant,' said Anda warmly. '*And* he saved my life.'

'Yes, I can't think why I bothered!' teased David and everyone laughed.

Suddenly everything fell back into place. It didn't matter whether Julienne was her best friend here. Everyone was friendly. Anda gave a sigh of happiness.

'And,' she said to Christie, 'I can do an eagle catch!'

'You can? That's marvellous! Come on then, let's get training.'

The day of the Club Competition dawned golden and still. Everyone arrived early to help get the hall ready. Lynne helped arrange the mats and chairs. Gran sold programmes and gave out numbers and chatted brightly.

Anda didn't feel nervous. It was good to work with friends, rushing to lift this and straighten that. She helped Julienne with the little ones, tying their hair and listening to their worries and hopes.

Julienne was nervous, as always.

'At least you aren't competing!' said Anda consolingly. 'It must be lovely just to do a display!'

'I wish I hadn't agreed to do it,' worried Julienne. She was white-faced. She was to do two displays of Modern Rhythmic Gymnastics, one with a ribbon and one with a ball. As soon as they had all changed into best display clothes, she started agonizing.

'It's the ribbon one that worries me,' she said. 'If you don't get it perfect it looks awful.'

'Well, what about me?' David reminded her. 'Doing a display in front of a load of strangers. I haven't even prepared one!'

'People forgive you if you make a mistake in competition,' said Julienne, 'but they expect perfection in a display.'

'Well I feel fine this time,' confided Anda. 'I'm not expecting to win anything. I'm just glad to be competing.'

Julienne looked at her curiously.

'Mmm—you always used to be scared!' she observed. 'Maybe Ian Barst has given you more confidence!'

'Maybe he has,' said Anda thoughtfully, watching Julienne unwinding the long golden ribbon for her dance.

The audience assembled, hanging coats on chairs and positioning picnic bags. Gymnasts rushed about doing last minute warm-ups. John and Christie spotted tumbling runs on the mats.

Anda lingered by the table where all the trophies and medals were displayed. How she longed to win one, but she knew she wouldn't. Not today anyway. She had won medals, but never a silver cup. Longingly she fingered the coveted Club Challenge Cup with its lists of names.

'I expect you'll be going home with that after your training scholarship!'

'Not today!' Anda turned to look at Lena. For once there was no animosity. Everyone knew Lena was likely to win the Club Championship.

Kerry was with her.

'Oh come on, Lena! Don't be catty. Anda's only just out of hospital. She nearly died!'

'I wasn't being!' Lena smiled. 'I wanted to be introduced to your dishy cousin!'

'What, David! Tough! He fancies Julienne!'

'He doesn't.' Julienne rolled her eyes. 'We're just friends!'

'Sh! We're starting!'

Christie came on to the stage with three important-looking visitors, two men and one woman.

'Who are they?' whispered Anda as the gymnasts marched in.

'The woman is a judge. The others are selecting for the county junior squad.'

'Oh!'

Anda's heart raced. The county junior squad. She did some mental arithmetic. Was she old enough? Yes. Just. Experienced enough? No. Christie hadn't mentioned it to her. It was obvious they wouldn't pick her. She wasn't even at her best today! Forget about it, she thought. But suddenly a huge wave of nerves washed over her.

'You've gone white!' said Julienne.

'So have you.'

'We'll look like two ghosts marching in!'

There was no time to giggle.

'Look po-faced!' snapped John. 'Everyone stand up straight. Tummies in! Off you go, Lena!'

Lena led the way in to the rousing march Christie always used. Suddenly they were gymnasts, po-faced and professional, not kids with feelings! Anda loved

marching in, with the parents clapping. Her nerves felt grabbed together, as if she had left her stomach in the cloakroom.

As they stood in an immaculate line, she studied the faces of the two men who were selecting for the county squad. Was she imagining it, or was Christie pointing her out to them? I'm imagining it!

'ANDA BARNES!'

She stepped forward at the sound of her name, as they all did, and presented herself. Bill cheered loudly. He always supported Anda vociferously and she always felt good about it.

The competition day began with Julienne's MRG ribbon display. Beautiful and elegant in a white and gold leotard, she danced and rolled, sweeping the glittering ribbon into spirals and rings. She looked marvellous, but Anda was not envious. Julienne had had a hard time in gymnastics. She deserved success.

'Brilliant!'

Anda gave Julienne a warm hug when she came back from her display, flushed and happy. She hadn't dropped the ribbon.

'Yeah! Absolutely brill!' agreed David. 'Really smart stuff!'

Julienne looked pleased.

'I'm starving now!' she smiled. 'I'm going to pig sandwiches and watch Anda!'

The two older groups were beginning with bars and beam while the little ones did floor and vault. Anda warmed up on beam with Kerry and the six others in her age group.

She didn't feel nervous. Or so she thought until she was presenting herself to the judge.

As she stepped on to the beam she noticed the two county squad men, their faces a blur, looking up at her.

Dancing and stretching, rolling, leaping and pirouetting, she went through her routine. Or tried to!

The fall from the girder had done something to her confidence. As she steeled herself for the walkover to back flip sequence, she had a sudden vision of London, its coppery sky twirling and the sound of Julienne's scream as the canal water rushed to meet her.

She fell.

'That's unusual for Anda!' said Christie.

Shaken and annoyed, she kept calm, getting straight up again. She took a deep breath. I *can*, she thought. But a shadow of pain in her head made her fall yet again, on to the blue mat. Humiliating!

'She's not right!' Lynne clutched at Bill's arm anxiously.

'I said she wasn't fit enough!' said Gran.

A wave of wanting to give up swept over Anda. Mechanically, she climbed back, but in her mind her legs were running out of the gym and across the lawn.

Silence fell as she balanced there, white-faced. Then with sudden kitten-like flexibility, she did it. A walkover and two flips. Shattered, she finished her routine and walked away, biting her lips, knowing she would have low marks and a time penalty.

Avoiding Julienne and David, she headed for the toilets and hid for three minutes. She stared at herself in the mirror.

'You will *not* fall apart. You will not,' she instructed her shocked reflection.

But her bar routine brought the confidence flooding back. She managed her eagle catch. And everything else. With Ian Barst's voice ringing in her head, she achieved a magnificent back somersault dismount from the top bar.

'Oh my God!' Lynne shut her eyes.

'She *did* it!' cried Gran, clapping.

Bill cheered, Julienne and David clapped like windmills.

Pleased, Anda collapsed on a chair next to them for a welcome break.

'You have improved!' said Bill warmly.

'Improved!' echoed Gran. 'She's made *strides*! Well done!'

Anda smiled, pulling on her track suit. She looked at her mum.

'Don't tell me, Lynne,' she grinned. 'You shut your eyes!'

Lynne nodded sheepishly, handing Anda a cup of squash.

'I just can't watch!'

'Anyway, I've blown it with that beam routine,' said Anda. 'I don't know what came over me.'

But despite that, she felt happy, sitting in Ferndale with her favourite people. And she had improved. Those gruelling weeks with Ian Barst had been worth it. And the beam work would come right again, she knew that.

So she relaxed and enjoyed the rest of the day. Her vaulting, Christie said, was excellent and gained her high marks. Her floor routine was snappy and beautiful. Claps and congratulations made a lovely change from criticism.

She gave a sigh of contentment.

The afternoon was nearly over. Soon it was time for Julienne's MRG ball display which she did with graceful ease. Then David.

Everyone sat up expectantly. Boy gymnasts were a rarity in Ferndale. Parallel bars and a pommel horse appeared. Then David came marching in, looking suddenly small and alone.

'He's scared!' whispered Anda.

'He's not!' said Julienne.

David managed to look very dignified. He began with a floor display. Not fast and brilliant like the girls, but slow, strong, and controlled.

'He's good!' whispered Gran, her eyes shining. 'I have two clever grandchildren!'

Next, a display on the parallel bars and on the pommel horse. Finally, David did two marvellous vaults. Everyone clapped and cheered enthusiastically.

'I never knew he was that good!' said Anda.

They made a fuss of David, who came back red-faced and bright-eyed.

'Great stuff!' said Bill, impressed.

David shrugged. But he looked pleased.

'They wouldn't think much of it in London,' he said. 'I don't often get clapped like that!'

'It does you good once in a while to get a bit of praise,' said Bill. 'I grow lovely beans and no one ever mentions it.'

'Oh, Bill!' Lynne started to say, when silence fell. The judges had added up the marks.

Quickly the gymnasts reassembled for final march in. As soon as they were all sitting in neat lines on the mats, an expectant hush fell, and the speeches and presentations began. Anda's heart throbbed. She tried not to think about winning anything.

First the medals. Kerry had one. Lena had lots! Time after time she seemed to be walking up for a medal. Anda looked enviously at her. She had *three*.

Then she heard Bill's loud cheer.

'Go on!' Kerry nudged her. 'You've got first on bars!'

Astonished, Anda jumped to her feet and walked out. She'd been too busy looking at Lena's medals to

hear her own name! First on bars! She'd even beaten
Lena, who was second!

Thank you, Ian Barst, she thought silently as she sat
down, happily fingering the medal. You did this for
me, even though I didn't like you!

But there was more to come.

Lena won the big Club Challenge Cup. Several
other cups were presented to the younger members of
Ferndale. Then Christie picked up a little bronze
coloured trophy of a dancing gymnast on a stand.

'And finally,' she said. 'We always present this one
to the gymnast who has made the most progress in the
past year. We call it the award for the most improved
gymnast.'

Kerry rolled her eyes at Anda and mouthed 'Lena
again.' Anda made a face. Then she heard Christie
saying:

'Anda Barnes!'

She had won the little bronze trophy!

'I don't believe it,' she muttered.

She smiled up at Christie.

'I don't deserve it!'

'You do!' Christie smiled. She put a hand on Anda's
shoulder. 'And stay here a minute—we want you for
something else.'

Mystified, Anda stood, holding the precious statue.
How super it would look in her bedroom! She beamed
across at her parents.

The clapping died away, and silence fell again.

'We'd like Kerry up here please. And Lena,' said
Christie. 'We've got one more announcement to make,
and then you can all go home to tea!'

Kerry walked out, looking puzzled. She frowned
questioningly at Anda. But Anda already knew! I
daren't think it. I daren't! Emotions flooded through

her. I shall cry, she thought crazily, if they've selected me. But I mustn't hope for it!

She dared not look at the two county squad men standing beside Christie. She hardly dared to listen to the long speech one of them was making about the difficulties of selecting the right girls for the county squad. And she hardly believed her ears when he finally said:

'And today we have been lucky enough to find not less than three of these girls in Ferndale. We have selected for the county gymnastics squad: Lena, Kerry, and Anda!'

Well that's it. I'm going to cry, thought Anda wildly.

The three girls turned and beamed at one another. They all cried. Then laughed. Then waved happily at the clapping people.

The clapping faded to a buzz of excitement. Parents mingled suddenly with the gymnasts. The golden sun of late afternoon glowed through the tall windows of the gym, and across the lawns of Ferndale.

Far away in London, the same sun lit the canal water as Moira walked home from work alone. On top of the footbridge she paused and looked down at the girder, astonished to see a small pair of shoes hanging there.

Anda's shoes, she thought. They'll be there for ever!

Women's Tug of War at Lough Arrow

In a borrowed field they dig in their feet
and clasp the rope. Balanced
against neighbouring women, they hold
the ground by the little gained
and leaning like boatmen rowing into
the damp earth, they pull
to themselves the invisible waves, waters
overcalmed by desertion
or the narrow look trained to a brow.
The steady rain has made girls of them,
their hair in ringlets. Now they haul
the live weight to the cries
of husbands and children, until the rope
runs slack, runs free
and all are bound again by the arms
of those who held them, not until, but so
they gave.

Tess Gallagher

Not a Bad Little Horse

MICHAEL HARDCASTLE

When the telephone rang late on the Friday evening and Rachel's father told her the caller was Kevin Huzzard her mouth suddenly dried up with nervous excitement. For Catch Boy was due to run again at Chesterfield the following day.

'Got a ride for you at Chesterfield tomorrow, if you're interested,' the trainer greeted her with deliberate nonchalance.

'Oh, great, Mr Huzzard! Absolutely great! Is it—is it—'

'No, sorry, Ray, it isn't Catch Boy,' he cut in. 'Bryn's still down to partner him. No, this one is in the first race, the one for amateur riders. Horse called Hay Days, trained by Billy Allaway. Mr Cayley's got a couple of horses with him and I gather he was the one who recommended you to Billy. Seems this is a nice sort of a horse but just a wee bit headstrong. Been out a couple of times and finished unplaced, run out of steam most likely. The thinking is he might settle for a girl. So what do you say?'

'I'm delighted to accept—and very grateful to Mr Cayley.'

'Good, good. Well, it'll be useful experience for you whatever happens. Don't forget to bring your riding gear when you come in the morning. See you then. Sleep well, Rachel.'

It was, as she'd expected it to be, a long time before she got off to sleep. The initial disappointment that she was not to ride Catch Boy quickly gave way to excitement. Hay Days, she decided, was rather a happy name for a horse. She'd never heard of him before but that wasn't surprising because there were thousands of racehorses in training. As she was riding against fellow amateurs the competition shouldn't be so severe. If she made mistakes perhaps they wouldn't be as noticeable as they would in a race dominated by ambitious professional jockeys.

Her mother, on hearing the news, had even offered to drive to Chesterfield on her own to support her. Rachel, though grateful that her mother had at long last accepted her ambitions, thought that wasn't a good idea. If she had a crashing fall or made a calamitous error of judgement she didn't want any member of her family to observe it.

The following morning was moist and misty and Rachel's first fear was that racing at Chesterfield might be abandoned because of fog. She listened to weather reports on her radio as she made breakfast but she learned little that helped to clarify the situation. In any case, local fog could disperse rapidly if the sun broke through and thus in such conditions no decision about an abandonment would be taken early.

At the stables she managed to spend a few minutes with Catch Boy while Nicola was with Zygomatic. It was Nicola's job to look after Catch Boy at Chesterfield

and so Rachel could concentrate on preparing herself for the ride on Hay Days.

Allen Smith had noticed the booking and had some advice for her.

'Let him know who's boss right from the start. These unknown quantities can be right tearaways, so don't let him get up to any tricks. Keep a real tight hold of his head, especially on the way down to the start. Then you're likely to come back together, not in separate pieces.'

At the racecourse itself more advice was offered freely by various envious stable lads, other riders and, more importantly, by Hay Days's trainer, Billy Allaway, a jovial little man wearing an outsize trilby hat. He had a trick of clasping Rachel's wrist between his hands as he talked to her.

'He's not a bad little horse, this one, but he's a bit green,' he explained in an earnest manner. 'I think perhaps he wants the gentle touch, the soft voice, and I'm sure he'll get that with you, love. You're really pretty to look at and I'm sure you've got a big, kind heart. I think this little horse was knocked about a bit when he was young and so he's liable to get upset if folk sound cross. So just take things easy, all round, love. All right?'

That advice seemed to conflict with what she'd been told by Allen Smith but she had to forget that.

'Very good, Mr Allaway,' she said politely. 'I'll remember all that.'

Nothing was said about the owner of Hay Days so she assumed he wasn't present. Doubtless, though, he'd receive a full report from the trainer in due course on her handling of the horse: and that would surely determine whether she was ever offered another ride for the stable. The fluttering of nerves in her tummy

wouldn't die down and she desperately wanted to
nibble some food to calm herself. Even though she
would have no weight problems whatsoever, for the
horse was due to carry 10 st. 7 lbs. (which meant
putting a lot of lead in the saddle pockets to make up
the difference between that weight and Rachel's), she
felt that it would be unwise to eat in view of her
forthcoming exertions.

Many racecourses still hadn't adapted to the
increasing numbers of women riders and so Rachel
wasn't at all surprised to find that the ladies' changing
facilities were in what was formerly a storeroom attached
to the First Aid Room. Such a location didn't exactly
help to settle the stomachs of nervous newcomers to the
chasing game! One other girl was already in the room,
and halfway through changing her clothes, but apart
from an exchange of greetings she didn't seem to want
to talk. Rachel was glad to discover that the room
contained a wash-basin but, predictably, no shower; yet
a shower was what she most enjoyed after a race whether
or not the conditions had been muddy.

She ran her hands over the woollen jersey, knitted in
the owner's colours of daffodil yellow, light blue, and
red, but before she put it on she tucked her back-
protector into place. The vulnerable spine had to be
protected if she suffered a fall and a horse kicked out or
galloped over her. All being well, her specially-
strengthened helmet would save her head from injury.

Before leaving the changing-room to go and weigh
out she picked up her whip: although she'd vowed
never to use it to hurt a horse it did help a rider's
balance. There was an unfamiliar dryness in her mouth
as she went through the ritual of sitting on the scales
while clutching her saddle and then making her way to
the paddock where the horses were already revolving.

To her delight, Hay Days proved to be a very good-looking deep chestnut with three white socks and a particularly luxuriant mane. He was being led round by a young lad and Rachel couldn't help wondering how he'd reacted to the news that his charge was to be ridden by a girl, and an unknown girl at that.

Billy Allaway touched his hat to her as they met in the centre of the ring and that gesture impressed her greatly. After all, it was usually the jockey who responded in that way to the presence of owner and trainer.

'Feeling a touch nervous?' he enquired with one of his widest grins.

'A bit,' she admitted.

'Just as it should be, love. That way you won't get too cocky and think you know it all. Now, Rachel, just remember what I said: take it easy and come back safe and sound. Bringing the horse *with you*, of course!'

She was able to laugh at that and by the time he gave her a leg up into the saddle she was feeling quite relaxed. The lad smiled at her, too, and wished her the best of luck. Nobody had said anything at all about the prospect of winning or even gaining a place. So she was under no pressure at all to achieve something in particular.

In any case, Hay Days was a long-priced outsider. The two disputing favouritism were Chapel Row and Vicksburg; the latter was ridden by the leading amateur, Jake Cooper, whom Rachel had met on her previous visit to Chesterfield. A bay called Ever-so-helpful was trying to show he'd been ill-named by throwing his head about in a very wild manner as he left the paddock. Rachel was thankful her mount was so placid; it was undeniably embarrassing to have to fight for control in front of such a multitude of spectators.

The weather had improved, but only marginally, for there were still mist patches about and visibility from the grandstands would not be good. Ever-so-helpful had calmed down by the time the ten runners were called into line and, typically, he was now showing signs of not wanting to start at all. In fact, when the flag fell and the race began only Hay Days was eager to get into his stride. That was just what Rachel had expected from the form he'd displayed in previous outings but she didn't see any point in restraining him. They'd both lose a lot of energy that way. Moreover he wasn't trying to run away with her. He was simply moving freely and apparently enjoying the exercise. Clearly nobody else wanted to make the running and so Hay Days built up a good lead before he reached the first hurdle. And how he took that hurdle would be the first real test of their partnership.

The chestnut approached the obstacle with ears pricked and giving no indication at all that it worried him. Plainly, it didn't. For he skipped over it as if he'd been doing nothing else all his life. Literally, he took it in his stride. Rachel was overjoyed. She stretched forward to stroke his neck and shout: 'Well done, Hay Days, *well done!*'

Hay Days showed his gratitude for such praise by, if anything, increasing his pace. Yet she had no fear at all that he was exerting himself too much at this comparatively early stage of the race. Nor was he threatening to run away with her, as he might have tried to do were he not in control of himself. The apprehensions she'd held about riding in this race were vanishing with every stride. Already, she was beginning to enjoy herself. So, too, was Hay Days. There couldn't be any doubt about that even to the watchers in the stands.

The next two hurdles were jumped with the same fluency and by now Rachel was wondering how far ahead of the field they must be. No other runner had loomed up alongside them; and, more astonishing still, she couldn't even hear the sounds of hooves or the shouts of other riders. Normally no race was run in silence. Jockeys were forever yelling comments to each other or asking for room to get through when crowded out and in a challenging position. But she wasn't going to risk a glance over her shoulder. She'd been told often enough how unwise that could be, if only because of the effect it had on a jockey's concentration.

Even though they were now in the back straight, heading for the two jumps that came so close together, the first sound she heard was made by the crowd: a collective gasp of disappointment as Vicksburg, the outright favourite at the 'off', made a complete hash of his attempt to clear an obstacle. As the horse sprawled and dropped a shoulder his rider, Jake Cooper, had no hope of staying in the saddle. Jake hit the ground, rolled into a ball to avoid as much trouble as possible and waited until the rest of the field had gone by before rising with a rueful smile. Vicksburg, quite unharmed, galloped on as though nothing had happened: and then, at the very next hurdle, veered sharply across the path of Chapel Row, whose rider almost had to pull his horse's head off to avoid a collision.

Completely unaware of this mini-mayhem behind her Rachel carried serenely on and approached the twin obstacles with confidence. It was entirely justified. Hay Days simply flowed over them like a river surging over shallow steps. Effortlessly, he was *still* extending his lead. Rachel continued to praise him at every jump.

Now, as they swung into the last bend of the oval circuit, she decided she must risk a glance to see where

the opposition was. To her astonishment, she saw that the nearest challenger (if he could be described thus!) was at least twenty lengths behind her. Yet there were only two hurdles to be overcome before they reached the short straight.

'Come on, Hay Days, we've got to keep going,' she said to herself as much as to the horse.

She'd heard of horses, and jockeys, who'd lost concentration just because they'd been out in front on their own for so long. Rachel was determined that wasn't going to happen to them. So far the chestnut had shown no signs whatsoever of running out of steam. He was galloping with all the relentless energy he'd displayed at the beginning of the race. For the first time since she'd set off from the paddock she had an inkling that not only could they win—they were going to! Her main concern was to ensure that Hay Days didn't make a mistake at either of the remaining obstacles.

The horse, though, must have known what was in her mind. For he treated both flights of hurdles with respect. There was no semblance of an error in his jumping and his momentum wasn't checked. Still there were no sounds of pursuit but Rachel wasn't going to look round again. Her only aim now was to keep the horse going. And it was only as the winning-post rushed towards them that, at last, Hay Days's speed slackened a little.

Only Chapel Row managed to stage something of a challenge and his final run took him well clear of the remainder. By then, however, the race as a spectacle was over. Hay Days had triumphed without really being tested or, of course, being shown the whip. In every sense, it was a bloodless victory.

Rachel, as she pulled him up, couldn't believe how

easy it had been. It was really only when she saw the stable lad's face, aglow with delight, and received calls of congratulation and even handshakes from other riders, that it sank in that she had actually won the race. Her first ever success as a jockey!

'Fantastic, fantastic!' Billy Allaway was chortling as he rushed out to greet her on the triumphal procession to the winner's enclosure. 'You did everything we could have asked for—and better than we could have asked for! Great, great performance, Rachel.'

There was only a scattering of applause from spectators for hardly anyone could have backed the 25–1 winner. The greeting as they entered the enclosure was warmer and Rachel happily posed for photographs with her winner. Several more people came up to say, 'Well done!' and one of them was Jake Cooper, apparently none the worse for his tumble from the favourite.

'Even if I hadn't been unseated I'd never have won the way you were going,' he said. 'I'm sure everybody else thought you'd come back to us, run out of juice, but this horse has obviously got ability and stamina. And you'd had the good sense to walk the course last time, hadn't you? So you knew what you were up to. I'm very pleased indeed for you, Rachel.'

There seemed to be so much excitement around her that Rachel had to be reminded by Mr Allaway to go and weigh-in: if she failed to do that the horse would be disqualified! As she left, after giving Hay Days a final grateful pat, she could hear the trainer doing his best to convince reporters that he had no idea the horse could win at all, let alone in that fashion. Later, when she read the sports pages, she was to discover how generous were his tributes to her abilities as a rider.

first peace

'i hope they realize that the olympics are dead'

anaïs nin, her clear eyes into mine,
and so finally after years of silence
i begin to speak out

so much crowding into my head to say, to vomit up
to scream, to cry quietly
and finally to accept and breathe deep
and feel the weight of it gone
and free at last

i have been insane the past years of my life
and am just now coming into my own self,
my own voice

i was the all american girl, the winner, the champion,
the swell kid, good gal, national swimmer,
model of the prize daughter bringing it home for dad
i even got the father's trophy

i was also jock, dyke, stupid dumb blonde
frigid castrating domineering bitch,
called all these names in silence,
the double standard wearing me down
inside

on the victory stand winning my medals
for father and coach

and perhaps a me deep down somewhere
who couldn't fail because of all the hours
and training and tears
wrapped into an identity of muscle and power
and physical strength
a champion,

not softness and grace

now, at 31, still suffering from the overhead
locker room talk, from the bragging and the swaggering
the stares past my tank suit
insults about my muscles
the fears, the nameless fears
about my undiscovered womanhood
disturbing unknown femininity,
femaleness

feminine power

Barbara Lamblin

Acknowledgements

We are grateful for permission to reprint the following copyright material:

Margaret Atwood: 'Woman Skating' from *Selected Poems 1966–1984* (Oxford University Press, Canada), copyright © Margaret Atwood 1990, reprinted by permission of the publisher.

Nancy Boutilier: 'Hotshot' from *According to Her Contours* (Black Sparrow Press, 1992), copyright © 1992 Nancy Boutilier, reprinted by permission of the publisher.

Julia Darling: 'Playing Pool', copyright © Julia Darling 1994, from *Sauce* edited by Linda France (Bloodaxe Books, 1994), reprinted by permission of Julia Darling.

Tess Gallagher: 'Women's Tug of War at Lough Arrow' from *Amplitude: New and Selected Poems* (Graywolf Press, Saint Paul, Minnesota, 1987), copyright © Tess Gallagher 1987, reprinted by permission of the publisher.

Sheila Haigh: extract abridged from *Somersaults* (Blackie, 1987), copyright © Sheila Haigh 1987, reprinted by permission of Penguin Books Ltd.

Michael Hardcastle: extract 'Not a Bad Little Horse' from *Winning Rider* (Methuen Children's Books Limited, an imprint of Egmont Children's Books Ltd, 1985), copyright © Michael Hardcastle 1985, reprinted by permission of the publisher.

Ernest Hemingway: 'The Big Catch' from *The Old Man and the Sea* (Jonathan Cape, 1952), reprinted by permission of The Random House Group Ltd.

Mark Jefferson: extract from *The Calypso Cricketer* by Mark Jefferson (Hippo, 1999), reprinted by permission of Scholastic Children's Books.

Glynn Arthur Leyshon: 'The Coup Stick' (The Ice Hockey Stick) from *18 Sporting Stories* (Galac Publishing, 1991), copyright © Arthur Leyshon 1991, reprinted by permission of the author.

Cynthia MacDonald: 'The Lady Pitcher' from *(W)HOLES* (Alfred A. Knopf, a division of Random House Inc., 1980), copyright © Cynthia MacDonald 1980, reprinted by permission of the publishers.